C0-AQY-570

EUCLID PUBLIC LIBRARY
631 EAST 222ND STREET
EUCLID, OH 44123
(216) 261-5300

Outlaws:
Dead Man's Hand

Also by Chet Cunningham in Large Print:

Outlaws: Ride Tall or Hang High
Outlaws: Six Guns
Battle Cry
Bloody Gold
Boots and Saddles
Comanche Massacre
Devil's Gold
Die of Gold
Fort Blood
Gold Wagon
Renegade Army
Sioux Showdown
Sioux Slaughter

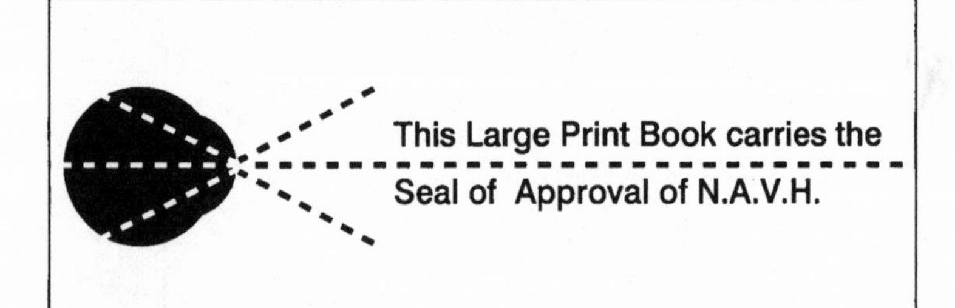

Outlaws: Dead Man's Hand

Chet Cunningham

Thorndike Press • Waterville, Maine

Published in 2003 by arrangement with Chet Cunningham.

Thorndike Press® Large Print Western Series.

The tree indicium is a trademark of Thorndike Press.

The text of this Large Print edition is unabridged.
Other aspects of the book may vary from the original edition.

Set in 16 pt. Plantin by Christina S. Huff.

Printed in the United States on permanent paper.

Library of Congress Cataloging-in-Publication Data

Cunningham, Chet.
Dead man's hand / Chet Cunningham.
p. cm. — (Outlaws ; 3)
ISBN 0-7862-5354-1 (lg. print : hc : alk. paper)
1. San Francisco (Calif.) — Fiction. 2. Gamblers — Fiction. 3. Outlaws — Fiction. 4. Large type books.
I. Title.
PS3553.U468D43 2003
813′.54—dc21 2003042656

Outlaws:
Dead Man's Hand

Chapter ONE

Winnemucca, Nevada: September 24, 1869

It was a crummy little flag stop town on the Central Pacific railroad line in the middle of a crummy little desert in the middle of Nevada.

But that didn't mean they couldn't rob the crummy little matchbox of a bank.

The six men in the Willy Boy Gang filtered into the Winnemucca First Bank separately. As Willy Boy came up to the only teller's cage he already had his neckerchief pulled up over his nose. When the surprised teller looked up, Willy Boy lifted his big .44 Peacemaker Colt from inside his long dark duster coat and aimed it at the banker's chest.

"This is a stickup! Don't move or make a sound!"

As soon as Willy Boy said the words, the other five men in the gang pulled up their masks and went to work in practiced fashion. The big man, Gunner, pushed two merchants to the floor on their stomachs and tied them hand and foot with strips of rawhide.

The Professor vaulted over the low counter and darted into the one office where the president of the small bank sat worrying over a ledger.

"Hands up on your head and lie face down on the floor," the Professor said politely. At once, he bound the man's hands and feet with strips of rawhide and hurried out to the large room.

Johnny Joe had vaulted the counter and tied up the teller. Juan had stepped to the door and snapped the night lock on to prevent anyone from entering. Then he ran with Eagle to the vault where Willy Boy had started pushing gold coins and silver dollars into a cloth sack.

They worked without speaking.

Johnny Joe brought in the teller's cash drawer and dumped its paper bills and coins into the sack.

Willy Boy stared at the stack of federal certificates which were known as Greenbacks. Often there was a big discount on the green money. He shrugged and stuffed a dozen stacks of tens and twenties and a thin stack of fifties into the sack.

"Any hidden drawers?" Willy Boy asked.

The Professor looked around the small vault with an experienced eye, saw a knob on a drawer and pulled it out. Moving with the knob a section of shelf came open revealing stacks of twenty-dollar gold pieces. They dropped them into the bag. Then Willy Boy nodded for them to leave.

In an ordered file they went to the back door. There they pulled off their long dusters and left them in the room before departing. Under the concealing ankle length coats they had on town clothes: two had on suits, another a jacket and tie, and three wore town pants and somber colored shirts.

Then they took off their identical black hats, pulled them apart, and pitched the black hats with the dusters. Each man had worn two hats. Now each had on a brown or gray hat.

Willy Boy checked the door, saw it was clear outside and the men walked into the alley, three in one direction and three in the other. Willy Boy carried the cloth sack of money in a large paper bag to disguise it.

They walked at a quick pace but without apparent haste. At the street, they turned back toward the town's main road and a few minutes later they ambled into the Winnemucca Hotel. Separately, they climbed to the third story and all met in room 312.

Just then they heard a shot outside the window and Willy Boy looked out. "Be damned," he said. "Looks like some excitement. One of them gents we tied up in the bank finally got loose!"

There were a few chuckles from behind him.

"Get the sheriff!" came the call from down the street. "Some gang of cutthroats robbed the bank. Must have been eight or ten of them!"

Willy grinned and looked at his men. "Gunner, you and Eagle stay here and watch the loot. We'll find out how much they figured out. Oh, remember, this is the only place we're together until the train leaves tomorrow afternoon. We'll meet back here tonight after supper to count and divide the loot."

The four bank robbers went down the steps of the hotel to the street and drifted toward a small crowd near the bank.

A paunchy man in his late fifties with a star on his chest waved the people back from the bank's door. "Easy, you people, easy," the sheriff said. "Me and my deputy are handling this. Mr. Wilson, would you come back inside so I can get your story with the others."

A man in a business suit and wearing a

green eyeshade nodded and followed the man into the bank.

"Heard there was ten of them robbers and they never fired a shot," one bystander said.

"I heard they raped a woman in there," another voice said.

"Wonder if they got all my savings?" a woman asked. "I had $87 in my savings account."

The crowd built and then dwindled, and built up again as the sheriff came out.

"All right," the sheriff said, holding up his hands for quiet. "They robbed the bank. Got most of the money, but not all of it. Mr. Jacobson says he has assets to cover his losses, so everyone's money is safe. Now, there were six of them, and they all wore black hats and long black dusters. Only trouble is they left the hats and dusters by the alley door so we don't even know what they are wearing now. The witnesses can't agree on what they looked like, either.

"Hell, the robbers could be anybody. So we watch for them. I sent my deputy down to the livery. Did anybody see six men riding out of town fast in the last half hour?"

The sheriff stared around, but nobody responded.

"Yeah, figured. Most likely they'll try for the afternoon westbound train. I'm gonna need me about ten deputies to guard every door to them train cars. I want to catch these damn robbers. Didn't hurt anybody, just some pride. Want every one of you to watch for these desperados.

"One of them is tall, well over six feet, two of them are dark, so they could be Indian or Mex. The rest of them just look like you and me. Goddamn! You men want to volunteer for an in town posse, come down to the office and sign up and I'll swear you in for two days. We'll check the morning eastbound as well. And then we'll just hope for the best."

Willy Boy grinned. He saw the Professor across the street leaning against the barbershop. At the mention of a Mexican, Juan faded into an alley and headed back for the hotel.

Willy Boy walked closer to the group and when the sheriff came his way he met his glance.

The sheriff paused. "Son, I'm sorry. I know you're trying to act grown up and feel like a big man. Fact is, you're just too young to be on a tough posse like this one. Maybe next time."

It was all Willy Boy could do to keep from bursting out laughing. Too young! Damn that was a gut buster. He turned away and looked at the window of the hardware and laughed as silently as he could as the sheriff and four men he had collected drifted on up the street.

Willy Boy stopped his laughter and turned back to the street. He saw a man coming and held up his hand. "The bank was robbed?" Willy Boy asked.

"Damn right! First time ever in this town. Must have been about ten of them from what I hear." The man was around sixty, with a craggy face and gray hair showing around his dirty gray hat. "Way I see it is they robbed the bank, now they'll try to hit a saloon or two this afternoon and when the five-forty steamer comes through, they'll take over the station, put a pistol to the engineer's head and make him take them past the next few towns for a clean get-away." The old man looked up and wiped his left eye, which seemed to be tearing con-stantly.

"Leastwise, young feller, that's the way I would have done it when I was a bit shorter of tooth."

He stared at Willy Boy a minute and the youth tensed. "Don't I know you, boy?"

Willy Boy shook his head and his hand swung down near his six-gun.

The man squinted his watery eyes. "Well

tarnation, I guess not. Thought for a mite there you was the spittin' image of my nephew over in Pocatello. Nope, guess not." He lifted his brows, nodded, and walked on by.

Willy Boy let out his breath, grinned, and walked the other way. These locals were strange people. He went across the street into the general store and bought a box of .45 rounds and watched the store clerk frown at him.

"Your pa know you buying pistola rounds, youngster?"

"Reckon he does at that," Willy Boy said. "See, he taught me how to shoot and all and it's his old six-gun he give me."

"Well, guess it's all right. Just don't want you to get all excited and try to shoot them bank robbers. They are vicious killers. Only reason they didn't hurt anybody in the bank was 'cause the president was so calm and dealt with them as gentlemen. Sure hope he can cover my account there."

Willy Boy gave the man a dollar bill for the .45 rounds and took the change.

"You be careful now, boy," the clerk said. "That six-gun there is a big one, ain't no damn toy."

"Yes sir, I'll be careful," Willy Boy said.

When he got to the street he laughed again.

Damn, but these Western people were dumb. Couldn't be that many strangers in a town this size, but they didn't even question him about the robbery.

Saying "sir" to the store owner brought back memories of his late father. Willy Boy scowled, remembering how his gang got started.

They had formed the Willy Boy Gang one dark night in Oak Park, Texas, when Willy Boy had pretended to hang himself, then overpowered and wounded the jail guard, killed two more deputies and escaped with the five other prisoners in the jail.

They stayed together after the break for support and so they could match the firepower of a posse that came after them. They shot the Oak Park posse to pieces twice and then the sheriff gave up.

But a week later, the famous bounty hunter Michael Handshoe and his own gang of expert shooters had galloped on their trail. They made three furious open warfare tries to shoot the six men dead. By then, each of the members of the Willy Boy Gang was worth $2,000 Dead or Alive. That was a $12,000 prize and dozens of bounty hunters looked for them.

But even the great Handshoe had to

admit that he was beaten and had to ride away for tamer game.

Even now in Utah the Wanted posters haunted them. A $12,000 prize was more than 28 years of pay for a working man who averaged about $340 a year.

The Willy Boy Gang had formed in the heat of escape and on the killing fields of self preservation. Three of the men had an executioner's black hood to face and the other three, ten to twenty years in prison. When they escaped they felt they had been grievously wronged by the legal systems. Now each would try to redress that wrong in the best way he knew how.

Willy Boy was chasing the bounty hunter who had walked up to his father's small farm and blasted him across his own kitchen with a bellyful of double-ought shot. The bounty man hadn't even asked Willy Boy's father's name. On a Wanted Dead or Alive poster, the reward was much easier to collect if a local sheriff would swear that the man was dead and telegraph the sheriff in the distant city.

Willy Boy's father was not Wanted, and when the bounty hunter saw his face, he knew it. So he turned the shotgun on Willy Boy, who narrowly escaped with his life.

He was an orphan, with a haunting

memory of the murder of his own father, and he was on his own in the Wild West. He found his father's big .45 and took it together with a sack of food and began his search for Deeds Conover, the man who had committed the murder. He had existed at first by rolling drunks in back of saloons, then he killed a man who resisted and he was on the road to a life of crime. He was in jail in Texas for killing a man.

Twice he chased Conover to ground, but the slippery man had managed to elude the final showdown each time.

Willy Boy would keep on looking for him until he found him, but now they were heading for San Francisco so Johnny Joe could meet again with the famous gambler Francis X. Delany. The cardsharp had conned and cheated him out of $15,000. The fact so enraged Johnny Joe that he swore he would come back some day and whip the fancy gambler at his own game. Now was the time.

The Willy Boy Gang was headed for San Francisco and a showdown in the heart of the gambling capital of the Wild West, San Francisco's famous saloons. This time the Gang would be there to be sure it was an honest, bare armed game.

Johnny Joe had been making his living

with pasteboards after a quick stint as a lawman where they tried to hang him for an official line of duty shooting. He had been in jail in Texas for shooting a man with a derringer when the other player accused him of cheating. The other player was unarmed. He died and Johnny Joe had a date with the gallows.

The other four men in the Gang had been in and out of trouble for some time, except Juan Romero. He had been in the Texas jail because most Texans hated Mexicans. Juan had been insulted and challenged to a fight. When it took place, he sliced up the white man who had goaded him into fighting. Only then did Juan learn that the kid was the mayor's son, and Romero was hauled into a quickly set up court, tried and convicted in one day, and sentenced to ten years in prison.

Anywhere but Texas he would have had an honest trial, but not in the Texas of 1869. Juan's cherished dream was to get back to Mexico where his wife and small son had gone after his arrest. But he knew he owed a loyalty to the Gang for a year. The Gang had rescued him from a ten year prison term. He could give the group a year of his time.

Willy Boy walked back toward the hotel. The Professor was probably the best man of his kind in the Gang. He was the oldest at 24 years, had gone to college for a year and actually taught school for a time. He was smooth and smart and deadly and could smile warmly when he killed someone.

The Professor was their expert with explosives and diplomacy and had been in jail on a bank robbery and murder charge that would send him to the gallows. The Professor was an inch shy of six feet, lean and trim and an excellent dresser when he had the chance. Now he sported a new silver vest he had picked up along the trail.

The Professor had as his one driving ambition to go back to a certain bank in Denver. It was at that heavily guarded bank that he had almost died when he stumbled into four guards on a quick robbery. It had taught him to check out any target bank carefully, evaluate any guards or presence of firearms inside, and decide if it was a good robbery candidate. That reasoning had paid off for him, but he wanted to even the score and knock over that Denver bank.

Gunner Johnson, who Willy Boy had left in the hotel after the robbery today, was the largest man of the group. He was a fraction over 6'4" and weighed 250 pounds.

Gunner had been jailed for beating up a

man in a bar who had insulted him a few days before at the livery stable where he worked. The big man was not dull-witted as many people thought, but he was a little slow at times and became confused quite easily.

Gunner was talented with all weapons, from his .45 revolver to a 10-gauge sawed off shotgun he loved to use with double-ought buck slugs.

Eagle, a full blooded Comanche, was the last man in Willy Boy's gang. He had been invaluable several times with his knowledge of the land and of fighting on the run.

He had been orphaned back in '63 when his father's band of Comanches tried to give up to Able Troop of the Fourteenth Regiment of Cavalry in Texas.

Someone fired a shot. No one really knew who it was, but at once there began a slaughter that ended only when every Indian was dead except one 12-year-old boy who had been out hunting. Brave Eagle was caught and sent to a Catholic Mission school. He quickly learned to read and write English, but the other boys teased him and ganged up on him. When he was 15, he ran away from the Mission, called himself simply Eagle, and began making his own way as a "White Indian" who could read and write English, but who also knew the ways of the Comanche.

He had been in jail in Oak Park, Texas, for stealing money from a Catholic Church poor box, and then cutting a deputy sheriff. He had been sentenced to ten years in prison.

Willy Boy detoured from the hotel and stopped for supper at the Great Western Cafe. He felt like he was starving. Robbing banks always made Willy Boy hungry.

Chapter TWO

The gang met that night in Willy Boy's room. They had the shade drawn and played a game of poker on the bed. Each of the men knew that tonight was not the time to be roaming and roaring around the local saloons, gambling halls and whore houses.

Johnny Joe laid out a hand for each and showed them how to watch for a man who dealt off the bottom of the deck.

"He'll be so slick you'll have to watch closely. The secret is to watch his fingers on the bottom of the deck as he holds them. He'll flip out a card so fast you'll swear it came off the top."

"Can you do that?" Gunner asked.

Johnny Joe took the cards, shuffled them, and found the ace of spades.

"I'm putting the ace of spades as the second card on the bottom. First the two of clubs, then the ace of spades. Now watch closely." He dealt out three hands of five card poker quickly. Gunner picked up his hand and grinned. He had both the ace of spades and the two of clubs.

"How you do that?" Gunner asked.

Patiently, Johnny Joe did it again, this time in slow motion, stopping his hands as the ace of spades came off the bottom and was halfway out.

"If you catch a man bottom dealing, try to grab his hand as he's moving out the bottom card. You've got to be fast, but if you can stop his hand the way mine is now, you can be sure he won't play in that town anymore." He chuckled. "Of course, you might also have a gun fight on your hands."

"You ever cheat at cards?" Gunner asked again with his open, anxious face.

"Seldom, Gunner. Not in a big game. I don't have to. The only time I cheat is when I spot someone else cheating. Then I revel in beating him at his own game, if we're playing each other."

"Anybody want to see how much money we made today?" Willy Boy asked.

"Oh, yeah!" Eagle said gathering up the cards and giving them back to Johnny Joe.

Willy Boy took the canvas bag out of the dresser drawer and emptied it out on the bed. The middle of the mattress sagged.

"Sort it out into stacks of coins on the dresser," the Professor instructed. Long ago they learned he had the touch for counting money and adding it up.

Soon the dresser top was covered with stacks of paper currency and gold coins. The Professor took the count of banded packages of bills from the bank. Most had written in pencil on them the amount they contained. He put down a row of figures for each denomination of greenback and when done went to work stacking the coins. He counted out ten for each denomination of gold double eagles, eagles, half eagles and quarter eagles. Then made equally high stacks of each coin.

It took him twenty minutes to list all of the coins and bills and add them. He made a quick second run through on the addition and then grinned.

"Not a bad little pile of change for a local bank. Seems to me I heard that this is some kind of special point for the railroad. They fix engines here or turn them around or something, so there's a lot of railroad money here."

"How much?" Juan asked.

"$7,422 U.S. dollars."

"More than a thousand each!" Johnny Joe said.

"To be exact, $1,237. Let me start counting out that amount into six piles."

When the money was divided, Juan asked to trade the others for the fifty dollar bills. He sent them to an uncle in Brownsville, Texas, who was supposed to take the money across to Juan's new family in Mexico. He was sure it was being done. He never sent more than $50 at a time, but mailed a letter at most of the towns they stopped at. Most of them would make it safely through the mail.

"How the hell we supposed to carry all these damn gold coins?" Eagle asked.

They all had bought money belts, but they were good only for the greenbacks. The gold had to be carried in a leather purse, a small sack of some type in their luggage, or saddlebags when they had them.

"An old gambler's trick might work," Johnny Joe said. "I knew a man when I was on the Mississippi River boats. He had a kind of saddlebag made that went over his head and had slots sewn in a pouch front and back. Each of the slots was big enough to take a row of double eagle coins. There was room for five slots and each would hold six coins, one on edge with the next. That was thirty coins on his chest and thirty on his back. He was a walking bank with $1,200 in gold in his vest arrangement."

"Too complicated for me," Willy Boy said. "I'll stick to a pair of tough leather pouches with drawstrings. I can still drape them by a cord one down my back and one in front."

"I'm going to get one of those vest things made tomorrow," the Professor said. "That is, if I can find a seamstress who will do it. Can the back of it be made out of some kind of canvas?"

"Should work," Johnny Joe said.

The Professor took a flask from his inside jacket pocket. "Freshly loaded with the best whiskey I could find. I move we all have a drink to our fine accomplishment today. Even more important, to our stylish getaway by completely fooling the local cowboys about who we are."

He drank, and passed the flask. Gunner grinned at them and nodded but didn't drink. He had told them the first week that any kind of liquor made him go a little wild. They didn't want to let that happen.

When the rest had taken a swig from the flask, Willy Boy got their attention.

"You all must have guessed we're headed for San Francisco. It's Johnny Joe's turn. We find out if this guy of ours can play poker with the best gamblers in the States. Which brings up the matter of the poker stake. How much will you need to get in the big game, Johnny Joe?"

"Not sure until we get there. It probably

has changed in two years. Last time I was there it was a couple thousand dollars — as high as ten."

"In one lousy game of poker?" Eagle asked. "With $10,000 I could go to New York City and live like a king the rest of my life!"

"It's not just one game," Johnny Joe went on. "It's more like a tournament, with several players, and some special rules, and then the winner makes a lot of money."

"Time limit?" the Professor asked. "Like you play for 24 hours, finish the last hand to start before the deadline and everyone goes home?"

"Something like that, I don't know what plan they use now. But I'm sure I'll need at least ten or fifteen thousand. I've got a little over $4,000 now."

"I can give you mine," Gunner said.

"No," Johnny Joe said. "I won't borrow from any of you. What I was thinking, maybe we could do a couple of special bank jobs and put the money into a poker fund. If I win we all split the cash. If I lose, then we all lose."

"Sounds good to me," Willy Boy said. He saw the Professor nod, and Gunner as well. Eagle scratched his head.

"Yeah," Eagle said.

Juan agreed with a grin, and it was settled.

"We'll have to do the bank before we get to San Francisco, probably before Sacramento," Willy Boy said. "I'll look at a map."

Shortly after that they all went back to their rooms for a long night's sleep. They wanted to stay sharp and ready for tomorrow. There could still be trouble getting on the afternoon train.

In his room that night, the Professor drew a diagram that he wanted for the gold coin chest and back pack. He set five gold coins side by side to see how wide they were and nodded. It was worth a try. He had almost $2,000 in gold and it was starting to get heavy in his carpetbag.

The next morning, the Professor had breakfast at the hotel dining room, then arranged to send food up to the rooms of Eagle and Gunner and Juan. They had arranged that the night before so the three men would have to be out in the town as little as possible.

The first seamstress he visited said she was working on dresses for a big wedding and simply had no time. The second one on a side street was delighted to make the device for him. He showed her the drawing and she nodded.

"I've heard of such things," she said.

"I carry rather large amounts of money for a business, and we're interested in some less noticeable way to move it. We think this would be ideal."

The Professor suggested canvas material for the backing and the lady agreed. He had brought along ten gold double eagles for sizing. And in an hour the pack was finished. Double stitching fastened a sturdy denim to the canvas backing and there was no sagging when one sleeve was filled with six gold coins.

It slipped neatly over his head and came low enough so it would not interfere with a shirt collar or vest.

He asked the lady how much it cost. She figured for a minute and looked at the clock.

"I usually charge twenty-five cents an hour, and the material was about forty cents. Would seventy-five cents be too much?"

The Professor said he thought that was fair and gave her a two and a half dollar gold piece for payment.

"It's ideal, and you've done a great job. A fine workman is worthy of her labors. The coin is for you." He thanked her again and walked back to the hotel eager to fit most of his gold into the holder. He figured it would weigh about five pounds when it was loaded with the gold.

★ ★ ★

Willy Boy came out of a saloon where he had been listening to the morning talk about the robbery. He had strolled down to watch the early train head out of town eastward at seven-thirty. There had been fifteen men guarding the train doors and the engineer, and watching everyone who entered. The same men would not be eager to be that thorough for the third time with the westbound that afternoon, Willy Boy told the Professor.

"In fact, I heard them grumbling. They said the robbers were probably halfway to Mill City on horseback by now. Three or four said they weren't going to check the afternoon train."

"Good. I'll walk ahead of you. I made my gold vest. Want to see how it works upstairs?"

Ten minutes later they met in the Professor's room and they slid in the gold coins.

"Let's just put in half of them on each side and test it," the Professor said. They did. It slid over his head and lay solidly front and back.

The Professor grinned. "Damn, I know it's there, it isn't like another shirt, but I'd get used to it in a half a day. Let's fill it up."

They filled the vest front and back while he wore it.

"And another thing, if somebody shoots me in the back, I got a gold vest on. That double eagle is going to slow down a lead bullet one hell of a lot."

When all the coins were fitted in, the Professor grinned. "At least I can try it for a couple of days and see what happens. Damn, I didn't think it would feel this heavy."

That afternoon a half hour before train time, the five members of the Willy Boy Gang drifted up to the ticket office one by one at the small Winnemucca, Nevada, rail station and bought their tickets. They waited outside avoiding each other.

The train pulled in from the east with a great squeal of steel brakes against steel, and then the gradual stop and the big hissing as the steam engine slowed.

This was a flag stop station. If they had any passengers, the station master hung out a two foot square red flag and the train engineer saw it and stopped.

Today there were about twenty people waiting to get on the train including a Mexican family. They lined up now at the two cars to get on the train. The sheriff came out and walked up and down the line of waiting people. He stared at each man and then moved on.

He watched Gunner for several seconds, and when Gunner saw him he flashed one of his near idiot smiles at the sheriff and a moment later the lawman moved on. Willy Boy had been passed by already and when the sheriff stopped near Gunner, the leader of the gang had his hand near his .45 gun butt.

This time there were no members of the posse watching the train. Just the sheriff at one car and his lone deputy at the other. The conductor came out and the people began to get on the train. The men of the gang split three and three on the cars.

Willy Boy was the last one in line for his car. He saw the Professor go on, then Juan was nearly ready to step up into the car when the sheriff hurried up.

"Hey, there, you, Mexican man."

Willy Boy stepped slightly out of the line. There were four people between him and Juan and the Sheriff. His hand was low and ready to grab his .45 and make big holes in the lawman.

"Yeah, you, Mexican man, hold it right there a minute."

Willy Boy tensed and let his hand rest on the butt of his lethal .45, his brown eyes suddenly deadly.

Chapter THREE

The sheriff hurried up, looked at Juan a moment and then reached down near the step of the train and picked up a letter.

"You dropped this," the sheriff said. "Didn't think you noticed." He handed an envelope to Juan and smiled. "You have a good trip down to Sacramento or wherever you're headed."

"Thank you," Juan said, took the envelope and stepped up and into the train car. He had dropped it. The letter was to his uncle in Brownsville and held a note and a fifty dollar bill.

The sheriff watched the other people as they went into the car.

Willy Boy paused as he came up to the sheriff. He couldn't resist.

"Sheriff, that posse you wouldn't let me go on yesterday. Did you catch the bank robbers?"

"Sorry to say, son, that we didn't. But we haven't given up hope yet."

Willy Boy nodded and walked on inside the train coach. Would he have a good one to tell the guys tonight in Sacramento.

The three outlaws who entered the first car walked back to the second one to find a seat. They sat as close together now as possible. Willy Boy had said this would give them better protection and fire power if they needed it.

The conductor told the men it was 178 miles of track to Reno. They had decided to buy their tickets only that far and stay there a day or more looking for the chance of another bank that might provide them with enough cash for the poker stake.

"We'll hit Reno slightly before midnight," the conductor said. "I'll ring a bell and let everyone know we're stopping there. I'll be sure to wake up you men who are sleeping."

Willy Boy thanked the conductor and settled down to enjoy the ride. The leather pouch of gold coins against his back grated and he shifted his position until they could fit under his arm, then he looked out the window and enjoyed the scenery flashing past.

"Damn sight quicker than riding a horse," the Professor said. They had reversed the seat so the two now faced each other.

"We might be doing more riding than we

plan on before this trip is over," Willy Boy said. He moved the sack of gold coins again. He was going to have to do something about that. Maybe convert some of it into paper. He hated that idea. Most places in the West discounted the greenbacks.

"How is your vest holding up? Any problems?"

"Not to talk about. I'd forgotten that I had it on until I sat down and felt it against my back. On the whole, though, I think it's going to work quite well."

There was no dining car on this train and the passengers all hurried off the train when it stopped in Mill City after a 30 mile ride. It was an official supper stop. Most of them ate a quick sandwich during the 20 minute time limit. There was no check by any lawman on the train and Willy Boy was starting to feel more at ease. They had gotten away with bank robbery again.

As they left the supper stop, Willy Boy reminded the conductor that he and his friend wanted to get off at Reno. Then he settled back in the seat and went to sleep as darkness closed in.

Sometime later, the Professor woke up sharply and stared around the darkened railroad passenger car. Something was different. Then he realized that the train was not moving. A few people were walking the aisle. He spotted the conductor coming down the narrow walkway between the seats.

"What's happened?" the Professor asked. "Why have we stopped?"

"Had a washout ahead. A hand car crew found it and a man ran down the tracks far enough and lit flares warning us to stop. Afraid we won't make Reno by midnight. Probably be more like noon tomorrow, so you might as well settle back in for a good night's sleep."

Willy Boy heard part of it, but he drifted back to sleep before he really understood it.

When he woke up, a few streaks of dawn were lighting the mountains to the east and the train was stopped. He roused, then came wide awake and looked at the Professor.

"Why are we stopped?" Willy Boy asked.

"Washout up ahead. Conductor says they won't get it fixed so we can get across before noon. So we have some time on our hands. Any problems?"

"I'd say we're free and clear on that last little adventure of ours. Might pay us to take a good look around Reno. Isn't the silver mining place near there, Virginia City?"

"Yes indeed, the Comstock Lode, richest mining area in the country, they say."

"Might be worth paying them a visit. Should be considerable money around a town like that."

When they woke up two hours later it was broad daylight and they and everyone else on the train was hungry. But there was no food and no chance to get any.

The conductor came through and told everyone the same story.

"We'll be here for another three hours until the repair crew gets the fill made ahead so it's safe to cross. Then we have another 25 miles to Oreana where we'll stop for half an hour or more so everyone can get something to eat. As you can tell, this washout has really put our whole schedule into a shambles."

A few of the passengers left the car and took a walk up to the washout to look at it, stumbling along the right of way. Willy Boy had no desire to see the problem. Instead, he sat and stared out the window wondering what they could do in Virginia City. It was a big gambling town, so Johnny Joe would be happy. But was there a bank there that they could take and still get out of town safely?

If the railroad didn't go in there it might be easier. They could get horses and saddles and do the job, then ride down the trail toward one of the towns and move over to

Reno slowly to get the next train out. He'd think on it.

Two seats behind him, Johnny Joe sat there remembering Francis X. Delany and his cheating ways. There was no assurance that Delany still had his casino, as he called it, or his big game, but the even money said that he would be involved in gambling somehow. He was too old to change his ways.

Johnny Joe remembered the first time he came up against the man. It had been on a regular poker table and the stakes moved up to where there was nearly $300 in the pot, which triggered a response from the house man who signaled for his supervisors. He called Delany over to watch the game.

The boss was always on the lookout for fresh meat for his big weekly playoffs which took $1,000 table stakes to get in. This was an open game and almost anyone who wanted to could play. The only rule was that it was not permissible to quit while you still had money on the table.

Only when you went broke with your table stakes could you get out of the game. It was a winner take all situation. If twenty men started the game on four or five tables, the last man with the winning hand won all $20,000.

It had been in one of these monthly $1,000 marathons that Johnny Joe had hit a streak of luck. He was playing as well as he ever had, bluffing precisely right, raising when he should, playing perfect poker.

He worked through the night and kept winning. Then with little more than an hour to go before dawn, he was the second to last man playing.

Francis X. Delany was the other one. They battled for 55 minutes, and then Delany won the last hand. He had cheated. There were five aces. Four of them in Delany's hand and one in Johnny Joe's hand. He had been so surprised at the winning hand that he failed to notice that Delany had an ace of diamonds, exactly like the ace of diamonds he held in his hand with his ace high flush.

In five card draw a flush with an ace high is a good hand, not a great one, but Delany laid down four aces.

If only Johnny had spread out his hand face up instead of concealing it. Then for sure one of the onlookers would have screamed about the five aces and Johnny Joe would have won. Then they would have examined Delany and found whatever holdout device he was using.

It wasn't until he woke up the next day

that he realized how blatantly he had been cheated. It was a $1,000 that it had taken him six months to save up.

This time it would be different. This time he would have five heavily armed men in the room with him to insure that it was an honest game.

Johnny had never told Delany what he knew; he had been too chagrined to mention it. But the hatred had festered and grew until it became an obsession.

He would beat Francis X. Delany at poker before he died!

Johnny Joe walked along the rails to the washout and stood looking at it with a dozen other passengers. Evidently there had been a cloudburst somewhere in the mountains above them and millions of gallons of water rushed down this small ravine and washed out a fill as the water swamped the six foot culvert.

He watched the men and horses and scrapers bringing in loads of rock and dirt to fill in under the ties which hung suspended by the rails which now supported them over a ten foot gap. It would take the men hours yet to fill the gully and pack it down and make sure it was solid enough for the train to creep across.

Johnny Joe watched the workers for a

while, then picked up small rocks along the right of way and threw them into the hole. Every little bit should help. He tired of that and walked back to the passenger car. Inside, Johnny Joe sat down beside Juan Romero.

"We'll be here a while yet, Juan. Want to play some Twenty-and-One just to pass the time?"

"No dollars?"

"No dollars, just for pleasure."

"You betcha."

They played the game for an hour, then tired of it and each took a nap.

It was well after noon when the train gave a jolt and then eased forward. The conductor came into the car at once.

"Folks, we're going to creep across the new fill and hope it holds. If it doesn't, we'll all have to walk to Humboldt, but that's only about ten miles."

The train inched along at less than a slow walk, and the conductor went to the first car to tell them the news.

"Now we're getting somewhere," Willy Boy said. He watched out the window as they came to the fill. The train slowed even more as the lighter rail cars passed over it.

"Damn near got it made!" somebody called. Then they were across the fill. The men with wheelbarrows and horses below on the right of way cheered and slowly the train increased speed as they rolled toward the first little settlement ahead named Humboldt.

They arrived about twenty minutes later and the train rolled slowly into the small village. The conductor hurried into the car.

"There's only one small cafe in town, but the owner has put together two hundred sandwiches and each of you will be brought two of them courtesy of the Central Pacific. We hope to meet our schedules and this was unfortunate."

When the train came to a complete stop they saw tables set up on the station platform. Heaps of sandwiches and large pots of coffee stood ready. The passengers hurried out and shared the food with the crew. The coffee was hot and black and the sandwiches were of four or five kinds from ham to peanut butter.

A half hour later the conductor called and the passengers straggled back to the train.

"Won't be long now," Willy Boy said as they eased into their coach seats.

The conductor came through and said they were still 140 miles from Reno and the engineer had estimated that they would be there in four hours and twenty-four minutes.

"That would make it right on to five o'clock," the Professor said and they all settled down for the rest of the ride.

Willy Boy was trying to figure where it would be best to rob a bank, Virginia City or Reno. It would depend how good the guards and town marshal or police were in the small town.

Reno had been on the east-west route for a long spell. The conductor came in again and told them about Reno.

"Just so you'll know and won't all ask me, I'll tell you all at once about Reno. The place started when a man built a toll bridge across the Truckee River at that spot back in 1860. Then he sold it to a man named Lake and in 1868 the Central Pacific got there and the land was auctioned off and we had an instant town.

"Reno is named for Jesse Lee Reno of Virginia, a Union army officer who was killed during the Civil War. We'll be at an elevation of about 4500 feet at Reno and in the foothills of the majestic Sierra Nevada range."

The conductor grinned. "Like to tell you more, but that's all I know about Reno."

Just before five P.M., the outlaws stepped off the train holding their carpetbags and straggled over to the closest hotel. There wasn't much of a choice. One hotel had three stories and a dining room, and the other had one story. They went to the larger one with several other passengers who got off there.

The rooms were small but adequate, and they wandered down singly and in pairs to eat in the dining room. It was habit by now not to function as a group of six in public. The practice had worked so they kept at it.

In the lobby, Willy Boy had picked up a broadside that called for miners or men with no hard rock experience to come to Virginia City.

"Plenty of good paying jobs in the mines. Safety conscious mine owners now hiring. Two dollars a day, six days a week!" There was a map showing distances and where to catch the stagecoach to get to Virginia City. The fare was three dollars.

When supper was over the men split up to go to their favorite recreation. Juan settled into a small bar where he felt they would serve him. There were many more Mexicans in this area since it once was Mexican territory.

Eagle wore his town clothes, no headband and lingered over the supper. He had two desserts, then walked the length of the city. He was not interested in gambling or drinking. He found what he wanted at the edge of the business district, a fancy lady house. He walked in the front door and smiled. Two women moved toward him with fake grins on their rouged faces.

Willy Boy set out $30 to gamble with, had a beer and played in a quarter limit game. Even if he was unlucky, it would take him all night to lose his thirty dollars.

Johnny Joe found the best gambling hall in town and showed $100 and asked for a game. He got one and figured that he should be able to win two hundred more before morning.

The Professor talked Gunner into coming with him.

"Look, we'll have a beer and then see what else we can find to do."

Gunner sat in the saloon and sipped at the beer, not really wanting it, but neither did he want to make the Professor mad at him. He was eager to leave when the Professor stood up. It was several minutes later that he realized where he was. The Professor had taken him upstairs to a nice parlor. Soon a fancy lady came in and sat down beside him.

Gunner's lower lip began to quiver. He'd never sat beside a woman in his life except his mother. He remembered her warning him to be extremely careful of girls and women because they had "certain equipment he didn't and it could be damaged easily."

Gunner looked down at the painted whore beside him and then shot an anxious glance at the Professor. The Professor was grinning. Gunner wanted out of there. But the woman had put her hand on his leg.

"Just relax, Gunner. This lady's name is Susie and she's going to stay with you a while. She'll be nice to you and do just whatever you want her to. Do you understand?"

Gunner shook his head.

"She'll explain it to you."

Then the Professor got up, took another woman's hand and walked through a door and down a short hallway. The woman who sat beside Gunner smiled.

"Now, Gunner, we can just talk or do anything you want to do. Should we go down to my room where there won't be a lot of other people?"

Gunner sat there frozen solid. He couldn't move, he couldn't think, he didn't even know if his eyes were open or not.

What in hell was he supposed to do now?

Chapter FOUR

Gunner Johnson forced his eyes open but he couldn't look at the woman sitting beside him. She had certain equipment he didn't and it could be damaged easily! He remembered his mama's warnings. What should he do now? Why had the Professor abandoned him here in such a dangerous place.

A woman!

"Now just relax, Gunner. I know you haven't done this much, but it's easy and you'll enjoy it, honest you will." She had stood and now caught at his arm to urge him to stand.

"Come on now, Gunner. Be nice to me and don't cause any problems. Just walk down to my room and we can talk. You can walk, can't you, Gunner?"

Slowly the big man nodded.

"Then come with me. Nobody is going to hurt you and you won't hurt anybody. We'll walk down the hall and sit in a chair. You can do that, can't you, Gunner?"

She watched him closely and he could see the swell of her breasts. They were part of the "equipment" he didn't have. He didn't want to damage them. He better go with her or she might be damaged. Yes.

Slowly he stood and the girl, Susie, smiled at him.

"That's the way big guy, good boy, Gunner. Now, right down this way and we'll shut the door and ain't nobody's business what we do. You just want to watch or to touch or just sit and talk. Hell, don't matter none to me. I got my two dollars. So come on, Gunner, right down here."

It was a terrible and difficult 30 feet for Gunner. He looked around to see if anybody was watching. Nobody else could be seen in the hall or the parlor.

When the woman took his hand to lead him, her flesh against his felt like fire. He almost pulled his hand away, but she smiled so nice he thought she must not be damaged. Anyway, she was the one who had touched him, so it had to be all right.

"Down here, Gunner. Where are you from? You're new in town, I hear."

"Texas," Gunner managed to whisper to her.

"Texas. Well, you're tall enough to be from Texas. Is that place as big as I hear?

They say you can ride in a stagecoach for days and not get across the place."

She held open a door to let him go in, but he just stood there. She caught his hand again and went in the room first and urged him to come in with her. After another hesitation, he followed her. She closed the door.

Gunner looked around with amazement. It was smaller than his hotel room and had only a plain iron bed, a small dresser and a chair. One window had a shade pulled down. It was on the ground floor.

"This is my room, Gunner. Not very much, but it's better than walking the streets. You want to sit on the bed or on the chair?"

Gunner quickly sat on the chair. Susie sat on the bed and watched him a minute, then she smiled. "Gunner, is it true that you've never been with a woman, never made love?"

The big man nodded slowly.

"Christ! I can hardly believe it. How old are you, twenty-two, twenty-three?"

"Twenty."

"Well, good. I finally got you to say one word. Are you afraid of me, Gunner?"

He nodded.

"Why? How could I hurt a big guy like you?"

"I might hurt you."

Susie laughed. "Not a chance, Gunner. You're a big cuddly bear who couldn't hurt a puppy dog."

"I might hurt your . . . your equipment."

Susie frowned. She stared at him and unbuttoned the top of her dress. "My equipment? I don't understand, Gunner."

"My mama told me girls have equipment I don't and it is easily damaged."

"Oh, my God. Some bitch of a mother she must have been. Gunner, most of what your mother meant is that women have breasts and they get tender sometimes. See, these are my breasts."

She opened the dress showing her breasts and Gunner's eyes widened in surprise and alarm. He jumped up, knocking over the chair and darted to the door. He fumbled with the knob for a minute, wrenched it open and stormed out into the hall.

For a moment he was lost, then he saw the parlor and ran that way, found the door and burst outside. Gunner ran for two blocks before he stopped. He was panting and heaving for breath. The stark, perfect image of Susie's two naked breasts had been burned into his memory.

Equipment. He shook his head. He'd never seen anything like that before. Equipment. Gunner walked quickly back to the hotel and went into his room and lay down on his bed and went back over the whole experience. Equipment. They didn't look like they would break. How could they be damaged?

Susie wasn't nice. She had called his mother a bad name. He wouldn't talk to Susie anymore.

Gunner thought about the girl and his mother. He missed his mother. Susie was a bad person. After a few minutes, Gunner drifted off to sleep and dreamed of his mother, of the good times when she took care of him in Texas.

Juan found a small cafe that served Mexican and American food. When the waitress came he almost wept, she looked so much like his wife Juanita. He spoke to her in Spanish. She grinned and took him back to meet her father. He also was from Texas and had come west five years ago.

"The life here is much better," Jorge Sandobal told him. Jorge was a large man with a sagging moustache and fierce black eyes. He was also a fine cook and now served tacos and enchiladas and refried beans to all comers.

For three hours Juan ate the kind of food he loved, drank tequila and spoke Spanish.

It was almost like he was back home. He enjoyed himself more than he had in months. It was nearing midnight when he said adios and returned to the hotel and sleep. Juan whispered a prayer for Juanita and little Ernesto now back in Mexico, then went to sleep happier than he had been in a long time.

The next morning after breakfast, they all gathered in Willy Boy's room.

"I went past the bank last night and this morning," the Professor said. "It looks mean and tough. I'll check inside when it opens, but my guess is that it's one of the better protected banks we've seen. It wouldn't be an easy go-downer. We'd have to shoot our way out. Not sure, but that's the way it looks."

"So we think about Virginia City," Willy Boy said. "Stage could get us there. Then we'd want to rent horses so we'd have another way to get away. Most likely we'd have to ride horses back over here to pick up the train on to Sacramento."

"We need a good sized bank or a payroll or a ton of pure silver so we can stake Johnny to that big poker game," the Professor said. "We might not like Virginia City and have to come back here and shoot our way out. Important thing is to come up with twelve or fifteen thousand for our player."

Johnny Joe was fidgeting where he stood against the dresser. "I'm starting to think this is asking too much of my friends," he said. "I don't see how I can ask you to risk getting shot in a bank heist just so I can have a poker game."

Eagle shook his head. "No, no, no, Johnny Joe. It's not just any poker game. It's your quest, it's like a young warrior going into the mountains with no food and only a knife to live for three days and find his life's quest, his purpose song, his guiding star. This, too, is something that you must do."

"I agree," Juan said. "We are bound together. We all have a second life after the jail, now we must help one another. If we can't do that the word friendship has no meaning."

Johnny Joe lifted his hand and started to say something else, but Gunner reached over and pushed his arm down with his big hand. "You play your poker game," Gunner said.

That ended the discussion.

Willy Boy grinned at Gunner, then looked at the rest of the gang. "So, our banker will check out the local possibilities, and then we'll meet back here at ten-thirty. The stage leaves for Virginia City at noon, which will give us time to get packed if we're heading that way."

Willy Boy looked at the Professor. "How is your golden bullet-stopping vest?"

"I forgot all about it, and I'm wearing it. Guess I'm getting used to it. Bank doesn't open until ten. I'll get in there and get out as quickly as I can."

A little after three that afternoon, the Willy Boy Gang arrived in Virginia City by stage. They jumped down from the Concord and were surprised at how big the town was. What had begun as a wild tent city in 1859 had boomed into an equally wild frontier hard rock mining town of more than 12,000 people in 1869.

The town was in one of its boom times when a rich vein had been cut into and was being worked 24 hours a day. The "blue clay" that the gold miners had sworn at and thrown away in 1858 now was a bonanza — with some of it assaying out at over $4,000 a ton.

The town was wide open with more saloons, whore houses and gambling halls than any city of its size on earth — or so the locals promised.

After registering at a hotel in their usual

manner, the outlaws split up. Willy Joe and the Professor each picked up change for fifty-dollar bills at the banks. There were two of them in the mining town's life.

The first one was sleek and plush and the Professor grinned broadly at first. Then he saw two men who acted casually enough, but were in fact hidden guards. Both had sawed off shotguns within reach and each had two revolvers on their gunbelts.

When he got to the teller's window he found a loaded and cocked .45 six-gun on the counter top near the teller's hand. He was sure there were more shotguns in the area ready for instant use.

The men both shook their heads when they left the Virginia City Commerce Bank.

"Looked like a fortress," the Professor said.

The next bank, farther down on C street, should be easier. It was not sleek and high class. There were more miners in the bank and fewer businessmen.

Willy Boy went to the teller with a five-dollar bill to get change for ones, and was quickly served. He saw no weapons of any kind.

Outside the Professor nodded. "That one we could do. No guards. Probably a gun or two around, but they don't have as much at stake. The Commerce Bank probably has $100,000 in the vault.

"This one, the Virginia City Bank, might have $10,000."

"All these workers banking wages got me thinking," Willy Boy said. "What about the payrolls around here? When do they pay the miners? Would there be a chance to get to one of those payrolls?"

They did some nonchalant questioning about when the miners got paid. Saturday night was payday. Today was Thursday. After talking the rest of the afternoon in three different saloons with miners and townspeople, they pieced together the target. The Buffer Mine would be the choice. They paid the men going off work at the end of the day shift. Buffer paid in cash, they had a pay office that was separate from the main office. Far as anyone knew, there were no guards around the pay shack.

The two outlaws walked up the side of Mt. Davidson and stopped a hundred yards from the Buffer Mine and spotted the payroll shack. It was not more than eight feet square, with a door in and a door out so the line of miners could continue straight through.

"We could ride in there just before quitting time Saturday night, blow the place apart, take the cash in our saddlebags and be halfway to Virginia City before anyone knew about it," Willy Boy said.

"Looks better than the bank. How much of a payroll would they have?"

Willy Boy scratched his head as they angled back toward C Street, the main thoroughfare for business in Virginia City.

"Well, we heard the Buffer had about a thousand miners. Biggest in the place. The men get two dollars a day, and if they are paid once a week, that should mean with higher pay for bosses and supervisors there should be more than $13,000 or $14,000 in cash in that pay shack every Saturday evening."

The Professor whistled. "Now that's a right respectable swag. I move we go after it."

The two had supper together in a fancy restaurant that bragged it had a French chef. They were still in their town clothes and got in the door past a cautious doorman.

The Professor settled in at a table with a fancy chair, a linen cloth on top and fancy table service with six knives, forks and spoons laid out at each place.

"What the hell is all this?" Willy Boy whispered.

"This, young man, is dining at its finest. French cooking in an elegant surrounding. What do you think?"

"I want frog legs," Willy Boy said.

"Good choice, I'm sure they have them. I want to see a menu before I decide."

It turned out to be the best meal that Willy Boy had ever eaten. He almost drew his six-gun when he saw the bill. Supper for the two of them cost over eight dollars.

"I coulda ate for a week on eight dollars' worth of grub," Willy Boy whined when they got outside.

"That wouldn't be living, that would be existing," the Professor said. "Let's find the others and tell them what you've decided about robbing the payroll."

Chapter FIVE

Friday, the outlaws bought horses and saddles at the Virginia City livery stables. They went in singly and were not overly particular about the horse and got the cheapest saddles available. They paid from $30 to $50 for the horses and five to ten dollars for used western style saddles, bridles and reins.

Each man took a short ride that day to get used to his mount and to learn any bad habits the animal might have. The Professor came back and made the livery man trade mounts. He didn't like the way the bay shied at every tree, bush and rider.

The livery man grinned. "Thought you might be back. I been trying to get rid of that bay for a month now." At last the Professor was satisfied with his horseflesh.

He bought a new vest, a fancy gambler's special with a built in pocket for a legal deck of cards. Johnny Joe told him few real gamblers ever wore such flashy clothes.

"It tips off the mark and the rest of the

players. Right away they're leery of you and won't even start to play. The secret is to dress simply, or just marginally average and lose the first three hands. Always works."

That night, the Professor asked Gunner if he wanted to come for a wild night on the town with him.

"You going to the same kinda place?" Gunner asked.

"Figured I might. I always have friends there. You could have friends there, too."

Gunner looked at him for several seconds then shook his head. "Susie called my mother a bitch. She is not my friend."

"Hell, she doesn't have to be your friend. Any of the girls will still do what you want them to."

"Not going there. I'm going to watch Willy Boy play cards."

"So nothing happened last night?"

"I didn't damage any equipment. I ran out quick so I wouldn't damage her equipment."

The Professor frowned. "Gunner, you and I are going to have a long talk one of these days. Right now I've got to hurry over to that house on D Street and see what I can find that looks interesting."

Gunner didn't reply, just watched him as he left Willy Boy's room. The rest of the gang had already gone. Willy Boy had heard the exchange, and would find out what happened later. He had a date with a deck of cards. He was learning how to play poker better every time he sat down at a table. Tonight he would risk $50.

Saturday, the Willy Boy Gang slept in until noon. In the afternoon they equipped their horses for a one night ride. If all went well they would be back in Virginia City in time for the westbound train at midnight. They bought three rifles and three shotguns at different stores and individually. Gunner bought a hacksaw so they could saw off the barrels of the three shotguns.

If it turned out they would not make the midnight train, they would camp out one night and ride into Virginia City the next morning.

Juan had set up his horse with a sack of food that did not have to be cooked. Lots of dried fruit, some fresh fruit, jerky, and two loaves of fresh bread. Each man had a small carpetbag in which he carried his extra clothes and personal gear. That now, too, was lashed on the mount just behind the saddle. Everything in the world that these six men owned was on the horseflesh ready for immediate travel after the attack on the payroll.

The mine work shift would be over at six o'clock and the men would come out of the shafts and line up for their pay. The Professor had decided it would be better to hit the shack at fifteen minutes before six. By then the payroll men would be in place waiting for the miners. More important, all the money needed should be there as well.

They mounted up at five-thirty and rode slowly north on C Street toward the far end where it petered out into the high mountainous desert. All six of them had changed from their town duds into "work" clothes that were fit for the trail and any kind of rough warfare they might get into.

They kept riding out C Street and then swung back, riding slowly. At twenty-to-six, they would ride up toward the mine, each coming in from a different direction. On their walk this morning the Professor and Willy Boy had seen no exterior guards. They didn't expect any tonight.

Willy Boy, the Professor and Gunner rode toward the north side of the pay shack at a walk. They were 30 yards apart as they started and now they angled toward the small building. They could see the other three men riding up toward it from the south and downhill.

Somebody yelled at them and the Professor called back.

"Special job for the boss man."

No one else said a word. A couple of miners heading away from the mine office waited for them to pass. Willy Boy and his two men reined up at the shack and ground tied their horses, then Willy Boy tried the door. It was open. He and the other two stepped inside and at once lifted sawed off shotguns they had carried against their legs.

Inside the shack, the two men looked up at them. "Wait outside, we're not ready to start . . ."

The man's face went white when he saw the sawed off shotguns aimed at him.

One of the paymasters had a shotgun but it was against the wall and out of the play. Both mining men sat behind a long white painted table that had a large cashbox at one end and at the other a written list of men's names and wages due.

"Boys, we come to relieve you of the wearisome task of paying all those men today," the Professor said. "Hands on top of your heads, *now!*"

"Never get away with this!" one of the men said.

Willy Boy lowered the shotgun and drew his six-gun, but instead of shooting the man, clubbed him across the side of the face with the barrel, slamming the counter to the floor where he lay groaning.

"Let's get the money and move," Willy Boy said. The three men unfolded flour sacks they had carried inside and began dropping handfuls of money into the bags. Soon they had taken all the bills from the cash box. They looked at the gold coins.

"Let's take the gold, too," the Professor said. "Hell, I'll carry all the gold."

When the coins were in the three sacks the men quickly tied a rawhide thong around each one, then looped the thong round their necks and tied the free end to the sack again. The move left their hands free with the money hanging from their necks. Gunner bent to the floor and tied the downed man hand and foot with strips of rawhide, then put a gag around his open mouth so he couldn't yell.

Willy Boy tied up the second man and gagged him, then pushed him to the floor. The three men of the Willy Boy Gang went to the door they had entered by and looked out. They could see no unusual activity. They walked out as if nothing out of the ordinary had happened.

Juan, Johnny Joe and Eagle sat on their horses almost against the side of the shack.

Their rifles were out and in their hands as if guarding the payroll.

"Who the hell are you guys?" a man with a rifle asked as he stepped out from the side of the pay shack.

Willy Boy hadn't mounted yet. He turned toward the man, drew his big .45 and shot the man through the heart. Two company men yelled. A pistol fired some distance away.

Willy Boy mounted and the gang rode downhill. Four men with pistols appeared in front of them. Willy Boy slammed one of them head over heels down the slope with a round from his shotgun. Gunner hit the second with one of two pistol bullets. The Professor had the wrong angle on the third man; he got off one shot with his six-gun, missed, and then rode the man down.

The surprised guard looked up and screamed at the last minute as he fired his pistol again. His horse's chest slammed into the gunman, knocking him down. The mount's back feet hit his head as the hooves swept forward. The hollow cracking sound could be heard as the horse swept past and the guard's head split open like a ripe melon.

The Professor heard the blast of the guard's pistol just before his horse ran him down. The round hit the Professor's left arm and it felt like he had been slammed with a two-by-four. For a moment he thought he might be jolted out of his saddle, but he recovered and fell forward against the mount's neck, hanging on and making sure his boots stayed in the stirrups.

The Professor shook his head, gasped in shock and pain and then slowly put his pistol back in leather. He looked at his left shoulder. Blood spilled from it. He couldn't even reach over to tie it up. He caught the loose reins and moved the horse closer to the others.

For a moment he lost the use of his left arm. With a great effort he lifted it from where it swung below the mount's neck and pushed it under his chest, then lay on it against the horse's neck. The Professor kept working his fingers on his left hand to be sure they would move. Damn poor time to be getting shot up, he screamed silently.

He had lost a few yards on the other riders, so he kicked his roan in the flanks to keep up.

The fourth guard survived the assault and turned and fired his six-gun at the galloping riders. He got off one shot, then the cylinder was empty. He swore and ran for a rifle.

The outlaws continued directly downhill

on Mt. Davidson and away from the mine. They had gone 50 yards when a rifle fired, and then another one. Now they could see five or six more guards with rifles who were running from a building.

The outlaws spread out even more to make them a harder target to hit. They continued downhill which was the quickest way to put the most distance between them and the long guns. A rifle bullet sliced across the rump of Gunner's big horse and it shrilled in pain but then only ran faster.

All six of the men bent low against their mounts' necks to make themselves smaller targets.

Well before they came to A Street where the silver kings had built their palaces, the Willy Boy Gang turned west toward the new road that led to Virginia City. This way they did not need to race through the town itself.

They skirted it high on the slope of Mt. Davidson. None of the riders was hit by the rifle fire. By now they had dropped down to hide themselves from the gunmen at the mine. They rode hard for another half mile, then curved down the hill around two more mines and onto the road north.

Nobody else tried to stop them.

"Willy Boy," Gunner said. "I think the Professor is hurt."

They slowed to a walk and Willy Boy moved back to where the Professor tried to lift away from the horse's neck. He pushed up with his good right hand.

"Afraid I caught one. Sorry."

Willy Boy grabbed him before he fell out of the saddle. They pulled off the trail in a little desert brush and got the Professor off his horse.

They took the money sack off his neck and stuffed the gold and paper money in saddlebags. All three money bags were emptied and the loot put in the saddlebags as planned.

Johnny Joe cut away part of the Professor's sleeve and looked at the wound.

"Damn, the lead didn't come out. All we can do now is wrap it up and get a doctor to dig it out tomorrow."

He had already torn up the three empty flour sacks into strips. He folded one piece and made a compress and put it over the wound. Then he wrapped the strips of cloth around the upper arm and shoulder holding the pad in place. He put three long strips around the Professor's chest and under his arm to make sure the bandage stayed there.

"We got any whiskey?" Johnny Joe asked. Willy Boy dug out a flat bottle and passed it to the Professor who took two good pulls at it and put it down grimacing.

He needed help getting his shirt back on, then started to stand. He slumped back down.

"Help me get on my horse. We got some traveling to do before them damn miners come gunning for us."

They rode.

Eagle held back as a rear guard and scout, but an hour later he had seen no pursuit, so he returned to the main party and they continued to make good time along the new road toward Virginia City. Far ahead they saw dust. It was getting toward dusk.

"Probably the daily stage," Eagle said.

They waited until the rig was almost within sight, then rode up a small dry ravine and waited for the coach and six to pound past them.

"No sense advertising where we are," Willy Boy said. He looked at the Professor. "How is it going?"

"Poorly, but I ain't dead yet. Never figure I'd be the one to get shot up! Damn! If I hadn't missed the bastard with my first shot he never would have had time to get off a round."

They rode again.

Darkness closed around them like a protective shell. Anyone following them now would be at a disadvantage.

"We keep riding as long as we can," Willy Boy said. "It's about 25 miles to Virginia City, and we might not make it tonight. We won't get the midnight train west. We'll ride until about midnight, which should bring us close. Then we'll take a rest and get the Professor to a sawbones first thing in the morning."

By the time they pulled off the road and found a small blush of trees and brush, the Professor was hurting.

"Damnit! Sorry to be slowing you down. When we going to count the money?"

"Tomorrow," Willy Boy said. "Now get yourself some sleep. We'll get that wing of yours back in action tomorrow. Must be a doctor of some kind in Virginia City."

Eagle came by and squatted down beside where Willy Boy was rolling out his one blanket.

"We need a guard?" Eagle asked.

"You think somebody is out there, tracking us in the dark?"

"Not a matter of tracking. This road goes only one place, and there ain't no stops in between. A blind man could follow us up this far."

Willy Boy frowned in the darkness. "Can

you stand guard tonight and still ride tomorrow?"

"Indian guard, Indian sleep. I'll go back toward the trail and put down my blanket. Then I won't be entirely sleeping but not fully awake either, a little of both. If anything big as a rabbit moves within 50 yards I'll be wide awake and aiming my rifle."

"Good idea." Willy Boy hesitated. "The Professor, how bad is that arm?"

"Not broken. Doctor gets the slug out he'll be fine in a week or two. He won't be the one playing poker in San Francisco."

"Yeah, right. That's good. Like to count that money tonight, but not worth the risk of making a fire. Hope the hell we got enough cash so it was worth our while."

"We did. Indian count . . . over twelve thousand."

"Hope to hell you're right."

Eagle took his blanket and rifle and walked silently back toward the main stage coach road. Willy Boy nodded. Now he could sleep with no worry.

Chapter SIX

Willy Boy got up a half hour before dawn and went to find the Comanche. The Indian heard him coming and waved.

"Not a damned thing all night. I'll get my horse and ride back two miles and see what I can smell or see."

"Good, we'll be moving forward at daylight, but probably not fast depending how the Professor feels."

A half hour later they were riding toward Virginia City. The Professor was hurting but wouldn't admit it. He ate an apple from the food sack and then a handful of dried apricots.

"I do think it would be good to move toward that medical doctor as soon as practical," the Professor said. They hadn't taken the saddles off their mounts. When the Professor tried to get on his horse he cried out in pain and sagged against his horse.

Gunner helped him get into the saddle,

letting him step on his back as a ladder.

Two hours later they came into the fringes of town. Eagle had caught up with them quickly that morning and reported no sign of any pursuit. Even so, they rode into town by twos. Willy Boy and the wounded man went first, found a doctor's office at the side of his residence and knocked on the door.

The doctor was a small man with extremely short hair and spectacles.

He saw the shoulder wound and motioned the men into his treatment room.

"Dropped my gun and it went off, Doc," the Professor said. "I know, a damn dumb thing to do, but that's the way it happened. I'm afraid the bullet is still inside."

The doctor handed him a fifth of whiskey. "Better have a drink."

"Take too much and too long to make me pass out, doctor. Just get out your probes and tweezers or whatever you use and let's get it over with." The Professor tipped the bottle and took three big swallows of the fiery whiskey, then wiped his lips. "Let's do it, doctor, I'm ready."

He wasn't.

The doctor's name was Cavanaugh. He cut off the homemade bandage and examined the wound. Then he moved the table where the Professor lay so the sunshine beamed down directly on the wound and adjusted his glasses.

He used a long steel wire probe and Willy Boy winced as the metal penetrated a half-inch into the Professor's upper arm near the shoulder joint.

The Professor's lips curled and his face strained and shook for a moment, then he gave a small sigh.

"He passed out. Now it'll be easier," the surgeon said. He probed deeper, then worked quickly.

After a few more moments he nodded. "Yes, I know where it is, I've touched it. Laying right beside the bone." He took a long handled, thin, scissorlike tool and pushed the points gently into the wound.

It was nearly five minutes, and a pool of blood on the white painted table later, before the doctor held up the .45 slug.

Without a word he applied some white bandage to the wound and pressed it hard to stop the bleeding. Then he brought some fluid in a jar and sloshed it over the wound. Next he put on some kind of ointment, applied a clean pad, and wrapped the wound carefully and tightly with an inch wide roll of white bandage. He taped the bandage in place and then put on another long strip of white adhesive tape to make sure the whole thing stayed where he had put it.

"There he is. Should do. He should come out of it in a few minutes. You be sure to have him come back here in three days, and then again in three more days. No horseback riding. Bed rest would be best, but that's a hard thing to make a man do."

He looked up. "You gents just get into town?"

"Yep, came up from Sacramento," Willy Boy said. "Figuring to do a little prospecting somewhere that ain't been dug out and overrun."

"Not many spots like that left here." The medic shook his head. "You kin try. Never hurt a thing to try."

Willy Boy gave the doctor three dollars. The medic handed him back a dollar.

"Don't hardly ever charge three dollars except for delivering a baby or cutting off a leg. Don't expect you want either of those services."

The Professor started coming back to consciousness.

"Best medicine for this man for the next 24 hours would be a glorious drunk. That way he won't feel the pain. He's going to have considerable pain for at least two days."

"We better find a saloon then," Willy

Boy said. "Any open this time of day?"

The six outlaws met at the biggest hotel in town. Willy Boy and the Professor registered there in one room. They took a sponge bath in the big crock wash bowl and changed into town clothes.

The other men drifted in one at a time during the next two hours.

"We'll leave our horses saddled and hitched in front of saloons and hotels," Willy Boy said. "Give the sheriff something to find and think about. Our horses still here, we must be here somewhere. All he has to do is find us. Only we'll be gone on the midnight train."

"How is the Professor?" Gunner asked.

The Professor had been drinking steadily for two hours and now had passed out on the bed.

"He'll be fine," Willy Boy said. He told them about getting the bullet out.

Each of the men had brought his carpetbag to the room and had emptied the gold and money from the saddlebags. Now they emptied all of the payroll cash on the floor and sat there stacking the bills and coins and counting them. Johnny Joe was elected as the best counter still conscious. He tallied up the numbers and added them three times. Then he grinned.

"Twelve thousand, two hundred and forty seven dollars. With what I have in my own poke that will more than make the $15,000 I wanted to have for the games in San Francisco."

"You're covered," Willy Boy said. "It's all yours. You keep it in your own duffel. It's your worry until we get into San Francisco." He looked around the room.

"As usual, we keep out of sight as much as we can until time for the midnight train. I'll go down and get tickets for all of us. Eat meals here at the hotel dining room or I'll have them sent up to the room. We just lay low for a while."

"The rifles and shotguns?" Eagle asked.

"Yeah, we normally wouldn't leave them in the boots. Bring them up here and we'll dump them here when we leave town. I want one of those sawed off scatter guns. Might shave the barrels a little more and keep it in my kit bag."

"Me, too," Gunner said. He still had the hacksaw.

The men went down two at a time and brought back the long guns and shotguns from the boots of their saddles. They didn't see any posse riding into town.

"What will they do back at that mine?" Johnny Joe asked.

"Hard telling," Eagle said. "It might even

be a different county. They'll put a posse of some kind on the road. Not a lot of different places to go. They'll know about the midnight train going west. I wonder when the east train goes out?"

"About now," Juan said looking out their third floor window. "The train just pulled in."

"Any posse of sheriff's men around it?" Willy Boy asked.

Three of them stood at the window watching.

"Don't seem to be any," Eagle said.

Just then they saw a group of fifteen men ride down Main Street. They stopped and the leader asked someone a question, then they charged toward the train.

"Got to be a posse," Willy Boy said.

They watched the men fan out along the three passenger cars and six freight cars. All but two of the freight cars had their doors open so they were empty. The posse men went through the train quickly. There were passengers only on one of the cars. They stood around waiting for the train to leave. Two late arrivals came and hurried on board, but not before the sheriff's men talked with them briefly. Five minutes later the eastbound train pulled out with a puff and a spout of black smoke. A low moan of the steam whistle and the eastbound was on its way towards Utah. The posse members quickly went back to their leader in front of the station and then they rode away.

A few moments later they came into Main Street, hitched their horses all in a row and began checking mounts along the rails in front of the stores and offices.

"Can all of you see your horses down there?" Willy Boy asked.

They crowded the window and heads nodded.

"Tell me if they stop and check out your horse," Willy Boy said.

Two of the six outlaw mounts were spotted and the posse leader, a tall man with a brown Montana rib hat, looked at them.

"They'll be checking the two hotels," Willy Boy said. "I'm going to go down and see what they ask."

He looked in his carpetbag until he found a pair of spectacles and a soft bill cap. He put both on and they dramatically changed his appearance.

"Now, I get to do some detective work on my own," he said. He touched the .45 on his hip, unbuckled it and left it in the room. He had a hideout derringer in his back pocket he could rely on if it came to that.

He walked downstairs, bought a newspaper and sat in one of the lobby chairs where he could hear and see the desk clerk. Willy Boy opened the paper and began to read. Most of the words were hard for him, but he understood some of it.

Before he was halfway through with the first news story, two men stomped into the lobby and went directly to the room clerk.

The clerk looked up. "Yes sir?"

The man he faced was six-two with a solid body, and about 35 years old. He wore a high crowned hat and a six-gun swung on his right hip. The bottom of the holster was tied down.

He glared at the clerk. "My name is Sheriff Lincoln Hillery of Storey County next door. Looking for six men. You have a bunch registered here late last night or this morning?"

"No sir, no bunch of six. Had four register off the midnight train from the east, and three or four more today, but no bunch, no sir."

"Was one of the men who registered an Indian, a Mex, or a guy at least six-five?"

"No. Three last night were women, and two today women. Can't count up six new men noway. You got any descriptions, sheriff?"

"Not much, just one big guy and one Indian and they thought a Mex. Hell, damn wild goose chase. They must have doubled back for Carson City. You be on the watch. We think we spotted two of their horses down in the street. We'll be watching those nags.

"Now I'm going to see your sheriff, Kitts. You playing games with me, little man, I'll squash you."

"No sir, no games. Just ain't anyone like that come in here."

The sheriff snorted and left the desk. He looked over the lobby, saw two men reading papers and turned. As he did, Willy Boy stood.

"Sheriff, what seems to be the trouble?" Willy Boy asked in his softest, most neutral voice.

The lawman stared at Willy Boy and his eastern soft cap.

Sheriff Hillery snorted again. "Nothing that concerns you, sonny. Just stay out of the way." He turned and marched out the front door with his deputy trailing him.

Willy Boy returned to his seat and laughed silently behind his newspaper. What fools some lawmen were. This one deserved to have his tail pulled just a little.

Willy Boy yawned, stood and took his paper with him as he ambled back up the steps to the third floor. The other outlaws let him in.

He told them what he had heard.

"Something going on down there," Eagle said. He had remained at the window.

They all looked. The sheriff had not mounted, but he had half of his men on horses. He gave one man instructions and the seven turned and rode back.

"He must be sending them to Carson City," Willy Boy said. "Good, it gives him that many fewer men here. We've got nothing else to do, why don't we tweak the sheriff's nose? I talked to him. He wasn't a nice man at all. The kind who likes to use his office to push people around. It's time he got a little pushing himself."

They set it up for dusk. Willy Boy and Eagle worked out the details. The Professor snored away on the bed, not feeling any of the pain that coursed through his body. All they had to do was get him awake and walking by 11:30 that night.

Johnny Joe wrote the note. He had a beautiful hand writing and had the most learning next to the Professor. When they had it framed right, Johnny Joe read it back.

"Sheriff Hillery. I know something about the payroll robbery at the Virginia City mine. I'll tell you what I know if you'll let me get on the train free and clear at midnight. The bastards shortchanged me. Like to see them rot in your jail. See me at the old stage barn at the corner of Main and Third at 6:30. You'll get more information than you'll be paying for."

They left the note unsigned.

Willy Boy took it down to the street, found a ten-year-old and told him who should get the note. The big man was standing in front of the bank at the time, his hands on his hips. Willy Boy gave the kid a quarter and he ran like his coat was on fire.

The sheriff got the note, read it and then evidently asked the youth where he had got the note. But when the boy looked around, Willy Boy was gone.

Back upstairs, Willy Boy and Johnny Joe began making the preparations. The other four men agreed to stay in the room and out of sight because the sheriff might stop them.

"It can't be too hot, that's important," Johnny Joe said. "We don't want to burn the guy. Hot, but not too hot."

They investigated the old stage barn and found a rusted out stove but it would hold a fire. Johnny Joe went to the hardware for what he needed and Willy Boy checked in at the general store for a pillow. They had what they wanted.

By six o'clock they were ready. At six, the other three men in the group had filtered out of the back door of the hotel and took up strategic positions near the front door of the old stage barn. They were well hidden and each had a rifle or pistol just in case the sheriff brought his men as backup.

The fire had been going for an hour now and Johnny Joe pushed his finger into the black goop and nodded.

"Warm and sticky but not hot enough to burn," he said.

They waited.

At precisely six-thirty the squeaky front door of the old barn sounded the alarm as it swung open.

Sheriff Hillery, with his six-gun out, stepped through the door. "Who the hell are you and where are you?" the lawman brayed.

Willy Boy stepped out from the shadows behind the sheriff at the side of the barn and hit the sheriff's gun hand with a two-by-four knocking the weapon from his hand. At the same time Johnny Joe darted in from the other side of the door and threw a blanket over the big man's head and tackled him.

A minute later they had the sheriff's hands tied behind his back. They put a gag in his mouth and blindfolded him. Then they pulled the blanket away and grinned at the lawman.

"What the hell?" the sheriff sputtered through the gag.

"Welcome, Sheriff. You're just in time for a little party. You're the guest of honor, Sheriff. Soon as we get you stripped naked, you get to find out first hand what it feels like to be tarred and feathered."

Chapter SEVEN

Willy Boy and Johnny Joe took out their knives and quickly cut off the sheriff's clothes, right down to his bare skin. They left his boots on because it was too much work to get them off.

Johnny Joe made sure the tar wasn't too hot, then began ladling it over the lawman's shoulders. As the tar took hold, Willy Boy cut open the pillowcase and pulled out the chicken feathers and pasted them on the sheriff.

They saved his hair and head until last, then carefully tarred him so it wouldn't blind him and then doused him with feathers. A second coating of tar and more feathers finished the job.

When it was clear the sheriff had not brought any back up troops for his lone mission, the other outlaws came in the back door and helped in the ritual. Juan had "borrowed" a saddle horse from Main Street, and now they tied a short rope around the sheriff's neck, the other end to the horse's tail, and walked both out to the street just before dark. His hands were still tied behind him. They took off the sheriff's blindfold and then whacked the horse on the rump.

The saddle horse pranced along 20 feet and then slowed to a walk, moving back to the home stable, wherever that was. The route led directly down Main Street.

The five members of the Outlaws ran up a block on the adjoining street and came out to Main Street before the tarred and feathered sheriff came by.

Already there were ten or fifteen young boys following the sheriff. Soon, late shoppers and some drunks from the saloons joined the parade, cheering and jeering and whacking the horse to move it and the tarred man along.

Two blocks up the street a deputy sheriff raced out of the saloon and fired two shots in the air calling for help and ran for the horse. He cut the rope and led the tarred man to the side of the street.

The Outlaws faded along with the crowd, then drifted back to the hotel to the room on the third floor.

By then the tarred man had been taken down to the doctor's office where there would be a medical washing off of the tar with coal oil and soap.

Sheriff Kitts stood in the middle of Main Street and bellowed out his challenge. "I want any man or woman who knows anything about this dastardly deed to come forward at once. We won't stand for this kind of insulting and criminal behavior on a visiting sheriff from an adjoining county."

"Was that old Hillery?" somebody yelled.

"Hell, couldn't have happened to a better victim!" another voice rang out.

Willy Boy pushed down the window and looked back to his own troops. The Professor was sitting up and asking for food. A good sign. He had a big thick head and a pounding headache, but his shoulder wasn't hurting as much now.

Willy Boy looked at the ex–school teacher.

"Think you can make the midnight train?"

"Does a whore have tits?"

Everyone laughed.

"I think he can make it," Eagle said.

The Professor had taken off his fancy shirt and the colorful vest that morning. Now he had Gunner help him put them back on. It took them a half hour.

Willy Boy put on his soft cap and spectacles and went to buy the railroad tickets. The train was on time according to the telegraph report. It would be in promptly at 11:45 P.M. for a meal stop, mostly for the crew, and leave exactly at 12 midnight.

By the time eleven o'clock rolled around, the Outlaws were strung out and heading for the train station. They stayed in the shadows and watched for the posse. From what they could see the posse was on a low profile of its own until the sheriff had completed his medical bath to remove both tar and feathers.

"If the sheriff gets any burns, it'll be from the kerosene washing, not from the warm oil," Johnny Joe said. "I've seen it done a time or two in the south. Getting that tar off is something like pure hell. Man never forgets it, I've heard."

When the train rolled in at 11:48 P.M., three minutes late, the Outlaws went on board singly except for Johnny Joe who helped the Professor. He was walking well but it hurt to move his left arm.

They settled in, three in one car and three in the other, all sitting alone by the windows. All wore their six-guns now and they watched everyone who came into the passenger cars.

The posse from Storey County did not check the westbound midnight train. It chugged away right on time, making several riders gulp their coffee and run for the last passenger car before it got out of the short station.

The train picked up speed and rolled along at its average of 25 to 35 miles an hour, and Willy Boy settled back in the cushions of the coach and relaxed. They were home free again, out and away, with nothing to stop them now this side of Sacramento.

Willy Boy went back to the second car and found the Professor where he sat rigidly in his seat. One of the saddle blankets cushioned his left shoulder and he couldn't stop the pain from spilling over into his face.

Willy Boy carried his carpetbag. He sat down in the seat facing the learned one and took a pint bottle of whiskey from his gear.

"Sir, you look as if you could use a nip of this," Willy Boy said softly. The Professor looked up, shook his head and glanced away. A second later he reached out with his right hand and took the bottle. He drank a quarter of it without stopping and handed the bottle back.

"Thank you sir, you know what a man needs in a time of pain."

They sat there a moment not speaking, then Willy Boy noticed a man coming down the aisle. It was the same deputy from Storey County who had been at the hotel with Sheriff Hillery. The deputy looked at each man as he passed, paid no attention to the women, only the men. He came closer.

Willy Boy signaled to Eagle and he came up to them. They moved back to the connector between the cars.

"It's one of the deputies from Virginia City. The sheriff must have put him on board to check."

"I'd suggest that we have a talk with the man when he gets here," Eagle said. There was an opening over the connector between cars.

"We're too close to Reno," Eagle said. "He could walk to Reno and wire the sheriff in Sacramento."

"We'll have to make sure he doesn't do that," Willy Boy said.

They watched the deputy working his way down the car. Frequently, he referred to a piece of paper he carried. He looked at the Professor but passed on. Juan and Gunner were in the car behind Willy Boy.

The deputy finished his inspection on the first car and came out the door of the first coach before he saw the two men.

"Sheriff, I have a problem," Willy Boy said as the deputy looked up. "This man is an Indian and he just threatened to kill me. I want you to arrest him."

"I'm not a sheriff," the man said.

"Of course you are. I was in the hotel when you and Sheriff Hillery came in looking for some men. I heard you. You've been with the sheriff all day. Where is he now?"

"He . . . he isn't here. I have no authority here other than with the warrant we have. I'm sorry. Now if you'll let me pass I have work to do."

"You still trying to find those men?"

"Yes, that's my job."

"Why look any farther? Aren't you looking for an Indian and one shorter man? Don't we qualify, Deputy?"

The man's eyes widened, then his hand darted to his holster. Willy Boy lifted the six-inch knife and thrust it hard into the deputy's unprotected belly. He ripped it out sideways and the lawman's eyes glazed, then drifted shut and he sagged.

"Over the side," Willy Boy said. Eagle caught the lawman by the arm and as Willy Boy wiped the blood off his blade on the man's shirt, they hoisted him upward and threw him through the opening and off the train.

"Never a dull minute around you guys," Eagle said.

"Life can get interesting. I wonder if there's another deputy on the next car?"

They went in and checked but found no lawman roaming the aisles.

The few coal oil lamps in the cars were now being turned down or out by the conductor. Eagle and Willy Boy went back to their own car and sat near the Professor.

He looked up and held out his hand. Willy Boy gave him another shot of the whiskey, and then all three settled down to grab what sleep they could on the rolling bouncing ride on the Central Pacific railroad.

The next morning at 6:12, the Central Pacific train rolled into the new railroad station at Sacramento, California.

Willy Boy came awake with a start, at first not knowing where he was or what was happening. His hand went first to his six-gun which was in the holster.

The Professor groaned before he opened his eyes. Never had he felt such pain as he had in the past two days. Now he knew why he liked to rob a bank without any gunfire.

Eagle had been awake for half an hour and watched the two white eyes with amusement.

It would be a breakfast stop of fifteen minutes. All of the outlaws got off and went to the small cafe on the edge of the depot.

Service was swift, the menu plain and simple with few choices, but the coffee was hot. Outside, the weather was also hot. It had been warm in Virginia City, but this weather was sticky so early in the day. The rest of the day would be worse.

Juan, Johnny Joe and Gunner joined the other three men and they stood and talked for a minute.

"We get back on and then we go right on to San Francisco," Johnny Joe said. "You used to have to take a boat from here on down to San Francisco. I'm sure the boat still runs from here, but it probably won't for long. The new railroad does the trip much faster."

The Professor felt better this morning. He'd find a doctor in San Francisco to take another look at his wound, and maybe even get some pain medicine. He'd heard that laudanum was good.

"Isn't that some kind of opium?" Johnny Joe asked.

"Sure, but if it kills the pain it's better than whiskey," the Professor said with a grimace.

"Who says?" Johnny Joe said. "I had a friend who had an operation and they used laudanum, and when the pain was gone, he couldn't stop using the drug. It took him a year to wean himself away. The doctor said he had been addicted to the stuff."

"Don't worry. I won't use that much," the Professor said.

"You won't use none of it," Willy Boy said, staring at the ex–school teacher. "Stick to whiskey, we know what to do with whiskey."

The ride on down the rail line was quick and uneventful. There was no word here about a small bank robbery back in Nevada. They stopped at several small settlements to take on and discharge passengers and freight and at last pulled into the new railroad station in Oakland, just across the choppy water from San Francisco.

"How we get over there?" Gunner asked.

"Ferry boat," Johnny Joe said. "It used to come every hour or so, half hour across each way. Don't know how often it sails now but probably at least that often."

"Heard so much about this place, but didn't think I'd ever get here," the Professor said.

"A word of warning," Johnny Joe said to all of them. "San Francisco is a fast town. There's a sharpie on every corner looking to separate you from your money or your luggage. Keep a tight rein on everything you own.

"The law here is sometimes so strict it's amazing, and sometimes lax. Usually, it's about as tough as the law gets in any big town. They have city policemen here and they can be mean. So steer clear of them. They won't bother you unless you get in trouble. They don't like a lot of shooting."

Johnny Joe looked around. "I can go on if you want me to."

Willy Boy nodded.

"I've picked out a hotel I've stayed at before. It's not the best in town, but neither does it cost five dollars a day to stay there. The fare used to be a dollar and a half a day. Probably about the same now. I'd be pleased if you want to stay there. I'm going to be on my own for a while.

"I need to re-establish myself as a player. That's going to take me a few days, maybe a week. Then I'll try to get in the next big game as soon as it comes. These games are the kind where they come to you and ask you to participate. You can't just walk up and buy in."

They walked from the train depot to the ferry without any problem and saw that the big boat was about to set sail. With a small rush all six got on board, bought their tickets and Gunner held on to the rail with a death grip.

"Never been on a boat before," he said. "Will it sink?"

"Never has yet, Gunner," Johnny Joe said. "This is as safe as riding your horse down the street. Let's go inside the cabin. They might even have something to eat in there."

The ride across the windy bay went smoothly, Gunner had a piece of pie and a drink of lemonade and before he knew it they were coming to the pier in San Francisco.

They looked up at the buildings as the boat nosed in toward the dock. Never had they seen so many big buildings and so many people. Men and women seemed to be rushing everywhere.

The dock was crowded with big boats from all over the world, their tall sails matching spaces with the lower, usually larger steamships.

As the ferry came up to the dock, men ran out with big ropes and soon the craft was snubbed securely to the dock. The gangplank was lowered and the six men of the Willy Boy Gang followed Johnny Joe down the plank and to the dock.

At once a dozen men pulled at their sleeves.

"You want hack, you want ride? Take you on ride anywhere for twenty cents."

Johnny spoke sharply and the young men pulled back, but ahead another nest of the boys and young men came out calling to them and shouting their fares. The cost had dropped to ten cents.

"We're walking," Johnny Joe said. "It isn't far and you'll get to see more this way. We have a lot of Chinese in town. The Celestials are everywhere, and very sharp merchants. They also cook and work for others, and they love to gamble. Without gambling I think the Celestials would just curl up and die. They will bet on anything, anywhere, at any time. There are gambling dens and parlors strictly for Chinese all over the city."

They walked down a broad street with trees planted in little squares around the cobblestoned street and sidewalks. Fancy rigs rolled along behind prancing matched steeds.

"This is one of the classy and expensive parts of town," Johnny Joe continued. "We won't be living here."

Ten minutes later they came into another street that had a mixture of hotels and business firms. Johnny Joe stopped outside one structure which towered eight floors high.

"This is your new home for a while. It has an elevator, just like the one in the Fifth Avenue Hotel in New York City. It works on the same principle as the Archimedean Screw, whatever that is. Come on inside and see if you'll want to stay here."

Chapter EIGHT

The first two days in San Francisco, the five members of the Willy Boy Gang did little but walk the streets, eyes wide with wonder as they took in the sights and strange sounds of the big city. Some said there were over 100,000 people there and more streaming in every day.

San Francisco was the cultural and business capital of the whole west coast. It was the jewel of the Pacific and the gold mine and silver mine rich princes were everywhere, flaunting their new found wealth.

After the first two days, the Willy Boy men split up, with Gunner and Juan prowling the docks and watching boats from all over the world loading and unloading goods. They had never seen such merchandise, fine china from the Far East, teak wood, ivory, strange fruits from the Hawaiian Islands.

Johnny Joe had warned them about the shanghai crews that went around at night filling out the contingent of sailors for the sailing ships. There were fewer of them now with steamships beginning to make their presence felt. But the shanghai teams were still out looking almost every night.

Both men were alert and did not frequent the docks or the saloons nearby after dark.

The Professor, Eagle and Willy Boy spent most of their time walking through the shops and stores. Anything made almost anywhere in the world was available to buy. They bought new clothes and small leather cases, and rings for their fingers and flashy new hats. The Professor now had six different fancy vests and he wore a different one every day.

Johnny Joe was working at his trade in the gambling halls. He quickly found that Francis X. Delany was indeed still in town and going as strong as ever. He was now 61 years of age and as sharp and quick as he had been 40 years before.

He now owned the El Dorado, one of the largest and richest gambling casinos in San Francisco. Johnny talked with a dealer at a faro table where he quickly lost $50.

"Yes, indeed, Mr. Delany is still fascinated by poker," the dealer said. "Was a time here ten years ago when poker was thought of as too slow a game for serious gamblers. But now Mr. Delany has his

$1,000 winner-take-all game nearly every night."

"Just a thousand?" Johnny asked as he won ten dollars back.

"That's the regular game. Sometimes on weekends he has the big game, by invitation only."

"What's the buy in there?"

"It just went up to $15,000. I've seen as many as 20 men playing in the game. They play until one man has all of the money."

"Is it still the rule that you can't quit the game and take any money out?"

"The same. One week a man won $300,000 for his night of work."

"Was it Mr. Delany?"

"Not that night, he wasn't playing. An attack of the vapors, it was said."

Johnny Joe won back another $25.

"Sounds like my kind of game. If you get a chance, tell him that Johnny Joe Williams from New Orleans is back in town and I'm looking for a good sized game."

"Yes, sir, Mr. Williams, I'll do that."

Johnny Joe was a ten dollar winner on the faro table and moved to the roulette. He had never liked the game because the odds were too heavy for the house. You had to pick one number out of 50 or 60. The odds were outrageous. Even the black or red was a fifty-

fifty chance. It was not a game for a gambler, but one for a man devoted to giving his money away.

Johnny Joe was moving around from table to table, playing for a half hour, losing a little or winning a little, and talking to the dealers. At each one he left his name and told them he was looking for a big game.

The roulette man was not so talkative.

Johnny Joe put ten dollars on the black and watched the wheel stop on the red. He put ten dollars on the red and it hit the black. He put twenty dollars on the black and this time won. He was even. So far he had lost $200 and talked with six different dealers.

The El Dorado was the plushest of the gambling halls he had seen. There were sandwiches and crackers and fruit on the bar for the taking. He nibbled at a sandwich and bought a beer and looked around the El Dorado.

It was simply the fanciest gambling hall he had ever been in. It was fitted with the best furniture available in the world. One whole wall was painted in fresco with a copy of a scene from a Michelangelo painting. Framed pictures of prints and oil copies of some of the most magnificent paintings ever made hung on other walls.

Huge windows with luxurious drapes were spotted along both sides of the hall. In alcoves, small copies of statues of the classics of Rome and Greece adorned pedestals. In one smaller room to the side, original sculptures by prominent San Francisco artists were shown.

Gloriously soft and luxurious couches, divans and lounges that graced the sides of the big room of the El Dorado were of the best workmanship and stylish fabrics available. They were further enhanced by heaps of soft cushions in crimson, gold and azure.

Marble topped tables spotted around the room held expensive vases of Bohemian glass of many hues, and of alabaster and artistic cut glass and costly porcelain. Fresh cut flowers were skillfully arranged by a gardener who would not tolerate even one wilting leaf.

Dozens of lamps and beautiful chandeliers graced the main casino hall, and they seemed to give off a softly conspiratorial light that sifted down to let only the winners see their lucky roll of the ball around the wheel, or the turn of a card.

Johnny Joe went to the 21 table, where the game was picking up the name of Black Jack. He bet twice, then asked the dealer if Francis X. Delany still owned the establishment.

"That he does, my friend. And a quieter, nicer gentleman I've never worked for. The soul of honesty and community service. He's a rich man, but still concerned for his employees."

Johnny Joe took another card on a total of 15 and broke. He turned up his cards and waited for another round.

"Is there still a nightly poker game for big stakes?" Johnny Joe asked.

"That there is, laddy, but you'll need a thousand of the best dollars you have to get in the game. They now take up to fifty percent in greenbacks at twenty percent discount. The rest must be gold, coin or dust."

"Afraid I'm not loaded down with gold dust," Johnny Joe said. "We don't have gold mines in New Orleans."

The dealer raised his brows and dealt Johnny Joe an ace to go with his jack of spades. He flipped his cards over and was paid double his $20 bet.

He won almost $50 at the Black Jack table.

"I'd like to get in tonight's poker game, if there's an opening. Tell your supervisor that Johnny Joe Williams from New Orleans is just waiting for the big game to start."

He worked two more tables, winning a little and losing a little, but each time making sure the dealer remembered his name and that he wanted to play in the winner-take-all nightly poker game.

He stopped at the bar for another beer, then ate three of the small sandwiches and sampled some of the small shrimp by dipping them in a bowl of spicy sauce. They were good. Not as fine as the Gulf shrimp, but adequate.

It was the afternoon of the second day that he had been playing in the El Dorado Casino before he had any indication that he might be allowed to sit in on the big poker game. He had gravitated to the poker tables in the curtained back room. The only requirement was that you had $100 in gold, then an usher opened a golden rope and Johnny Joe walked through. There were only two games in progress and ten silent tables. He watched one game with four men and when the hand was over stood behind an empty chair.

"Fresh money, gentlemen?" he asked, clinking a ten stack of double eagles back and forth from one hand to the other.

"Yes indeed," a tall slender man said. The others shrugged.

In this game you bought chips from the house banker who did not play. There was no house dealer.

"The house takes ten percent on chips," the cashier said.

He bought two hundred dollars' worth and got chips worth a hundred and eighty.

"Five dollar ante," the dealer said and the game of draw poker got underway. "Jacks or better to open," the dealer said. Nobody could open. They sweetened the pot with another five dollar chip each and the deal passed to the next man who kept the openers at a pair of jacks.

One man opened for five dollars. Johnny Joe contributed and asked for two cards. He wound up with a pair of eights and an ace high. He folded on the first round of betting. Three men stayed in the pot and it went to three rounds of betting. The opener won with his pair of jacks and treys to beat a man with pairs of tens and sixes. There was about $139 in the pot.

Johnny Joe folded on the next game as well, to establish his first two lost hands ritual. Then he began playing poker. He folded on the next hand, but won the fourth on a drawn third ace. There was $180 in the pot and he was ahead.

They played for an hour. Two of the men dropped out. Two men came over from the other game, and when the four men at the table decided to end it three hours later,

Johnny Joe was over $600 ahead.

He cashed in his poker chips with the cashier at the table. The chips were used only for poker. The rest of the casino operated strictly with gold coins and discounted paper money.

Johnny Joe accepted only gold when he was paid off. He had two pounds of new gold in his pockets, and felt like a walking pack horse.

"Is there a game tonight?" Johnny Joe asked the cashier.

The man looked at him. "You the guy from New Orleans?"

"Yes. My name is Johnny Joe Williams."

"That's the one I've heard about. I think I can get you in. You have the thousand in gold?"

"Yes."

"Game starts at eight o'clock. I'd suggest you eat a big meal before you come and drink very little. Once you sit down at the table, you can't leave. A good bladder is an advantage in these games. Tonight is a big night. We should have 13 to 15 players."

"How long will the game last?"

"Until there's one winner. It could be four hours. More likely it will run seven or eight hours. Tonight, Mr. Delany is going to play. Everyone wants to beat him."

"Where is the game held?"

"In the private salon, upstairs and in back. Over at that stairway."

"Could I look at it?"

"Not until time for the game to start, it's a house rule."

"Right. Are there many house rules?"

"No more than five to a game, no leaving the table. Paper money discounted 20 percent, winner take all. Those are the only rules."

"How often does Mr. Delany win?"

The cashier looked up at him quickly. "Not often, but enough to keep him interested."

"I hear there is sometimes a weekend game for big money."

"True, but only when there is enough interest in it."

"I'm interested. You might tell Mr. Delany I came all the way from New Orleans to play in his weekend game. I would hope it will be soon. I hear the buy in on that game is now $20,000."

Again the cashier looked up and frowned. "No, not that I know of. It's been $15,000 for almost a year now. I'll tell Mr. Delany of your interest."

It was five-thirty. Johnny Joe walked out of the El Dorado and down the street to Delmonico's Restaurant. It was a copy of the famous eatery in New York, but neither the decor nor the food was as good.

Johnny Joe had a 16-ounce steak and all the trimmings, drank no coffee and ate four thick slices of bread to help absorb the moisture in his stomach. He was not a man with a bladder problem, but the bread would help. At least that's what a gambler friend of his on the boats used to say.

After the dinner, he took a casual walk up and down and around Portsmouth Square, which had been the main central plaza of the town in the Mexican days. Now it was surrounded by some of the biggest and richest of the gambling halls and casinos in San Francisco.

He passed a policeman who nodded at him. Johnny Joe was walking carefully so his pockets full of double eagles wouldn't swing back and forth.

At the casino he sat on one of the sofas and watched the clientele. There were high rollers in top hats at the gaming tables. Right beside them might be a miner fresh off the diggings with a slouch hat and dust still on his jeans and mud on his boots.

Everyone was treated alike in the gambling halls. San Francisco had a large population of Chinese, some said over 20,000. They were furious gamblers and welcome at any of the casinos. Now and again a black face showed in the halls and frequently there were Mexicans, some shrouded in blankets.

As he looked around he spotted half a dozen women who usually were with a man and gambling for all their purse was worth.

The bar at the El Dorado was worked by three barmaids. It gave a perky, pleasant atmosphere to the mostly male house.

A five piece orchestra was assembled on a small balcony at the far end of the hall. They were advertised that they would play operatic music.

Now the entire hall, perhaps 70 feet long and 50 feet wide, probably held more than 200 people, many standing shoulder to shoulder around the tables. But there was little talk except for a low murmur at the tables. The most noticeable sound was the constant clinking of gold coins as the gamblers shuffled them from one hand to another while waiting to bet or figuring out which number or card to select.

Johnny Joe had two more of the small sandwiches but no beer as he girded for the long haul. It had been some time since he had played poker straight for eight hours. But he was ready. This was not the big money making game, this was the qualifying run to show Delany that he could play the game. Johnny Joe was sure that the big gambler man did not remember him from two years ago. He had cheated too many other men by this time to remember one who had made no trouble when he should have.

When Johnny Joe arrived at the steps toward the upstairs poker parlor, he was approached by the cashier he had talked to before.

"Mr. Williams, good to see you. We've kept a seat for you upstairs. This is where you buy your chips."

Johnny Joe dug out the 50 gold double eagles, received his stacks of pre-counted chips and climbed the steps looking forward to his first big game in over two years.

Chapter NINE

At the top of the steps, Johnny Joe found a large pleasant parlor type room. It had five poker tables spaced around with five chairs at each one. Half a dozen men stood talking. One had a drink, but the rest smoked or just listened.

Each of the men held his quota of chips. They glanced up at Johnny as he came into the room but made no move to say hello or include him in their circle. Some of the men knew each other and were at ease that way.

Johnny Joe sat down at one of the tables, stacked his chips in front of him and waited.

Ten minutes later there were nine men in the room, then two more came and then one more.

The cashier stepped into the room.

"Mr. Delany wishes me to express his regrets but a business meeting will prevent him from enjoying your company tonight. He wishes you all good luck. I will be the moderator and all disputes of any kind will be settled by me. Are there any questions?"

The cashier waited a moment but no one spoke.

"Very well. Let's use the tables at each end of the room, which will give you a little separation. We have twelve players. Let's make it two tables of six, that will bring the action a bit faster. Is there any objection to that?"

Again no one spoke.

"Please find your places and then I'll go over the rules."

When the men had settled into two groups of six around the tables, the cashier went through the rules.

"Regular casino poker. Standard rules. No crazy games or wild cards. Dealer calls the game. Standard ante is ten dollars, no deviation. No progressive openers. Table stakes only of $1,000. No one may leave the room and remain in the game.

"When a player cannot meet a bet or a raise, he is eliminated and must leave the room within two minutes. No player may quit and take money out of the room. When a table gets down to two players those two will move to the other table regardless of how many players it has. The last two players left in the game may play off the match with any poker game except five or seven card showdown. Winner takes all. No player can go light on a pot.

"Any player may call for a new deck or a card count at any time. That's my job. In such a case, all players' hands will be on top of the table at all times. Beverages will be served on call, but no food is allowed. If you don't remember the rules they are printed on a small card glued to the table at each position. I'm breaking the seal on these two new decks of cards."

He lay a deck on each table. "Cut cards for deal and begin play now."

As he waited for the cards, Johnny Joe had been evaluating the players at his table. The man on his left had a town suit and diamond stick pin, ruffled shirt and a diamond ring on his finger. He was about 50. He would play close to his vest, never bluff, show a good hand by his expression and be easy to bluff.

The man next to him wore a black suit, white shirt and a string tie but wasn't comfortable. He probably was a miner in from the hills determined to spend his money as fast as he could. He was in his late 20's and would not be any trouble, a splurger, a plunger and a bluffer.

The third man around the table was small and lean, about 35. He had the look of an experienced man, a gambler by trade. This would be nothing but an exercise for him to get in the bigger game. An excellent player, studied bluffer, good at figuring the odds of cards showing in a six player game. A worthy opponent who would not be above cheating to win. A 'watch-him' player.

The fourth man was older, in his late 60's. Quietly rich, here for the entertainment, the money meant nothing. Winning was not that important, the thrill of the game was more to the point. If he got a lucky streak going he would be tough. Otherwise, no problem.

The man to Johnny Joe's right was in his 30's. When his cards came he picked them up all at once, spread them in one move and checked them quickly. Another professional, but this one had more flash than substance. Maybe a former dealer out on his own. Lots of bluff. Still learning to be a big league player. Not a cheater, he would learn. Not a big threat.

No names were used.

The first hand dealt came from the thin, dark eyed professional. He dealt quickly and Johnny Joe watched closely and saw no move to bottom deal. Five card draw.

"Jacks or better," the dealer said.

Out of six hands there would be openers. There were.

The third man around the circle opened for $20. Everyone stayed in. Johnny had a pair of threes, a king, ace and a four. He discarded three and held the pair trying for another trey.

The older man took only two cards, the rest three. Johnny Joe watched the dealer carefully. He would be pristine pure this early in the game but there could be some indications. Nothing out of the norm happened.

"Opener bets," the dealer rasped when the miner didn't respond at once.

"Oh, uh . . . ten dollars."

The lean gambler directly across the table from Johnny Joe flicked out a ten dollar chip automatically.

The older man threw in his cards face down into the pot. The new professional tossed in a chip and Johnny Joe picked up three of the ten dollar chips.

"Ten and bump it up twenty," he said, his voice flat. The dark eyed gambler looked up at him quickly, then away. The man with the diamond stick pin and ring looked at Johnny Joe, shrugged, and put in the thirty he owed the pot.

The opener man stayed, the gambler threw in his cards and so did the new professional.

That left Johnny Joe, the miner and the diamond stick pin man.

"Let's see them, you're called," the man in his 50's said.

Johnny Joe laid down three treys and the other men still in the game groaned and threw in their hands face down. Johnny Joe pulled in the pot of about a hundred and fifty. Probably the smallest pot of the night.

The cards went around to the man in his 60's who shuffled them three times, then dealt. Johnny Joe anted and watched the hands work the cards. There was no chance this man would be bottom dealing, he moved too slow to cover it. Besides, it was too early in the game for any of the players to have anything set up unless they came with a whole deck up their sleeve.

The second game went smooth enough. Another straight draw poker that nobody could open. On the next hand, the oldest man opened and won the pot.

The third game was named as five card stud by Johnny Joe. It is a bluffer's delight, with two cards dealt down to each player, then one card up around the circle. The high card showing bet. Johnny Joe often used it early in a game to get an idea how different men bet when there were no draw cards. Johnny Joe pulled an ace for his up card with a three and a two in the hole. He bet $20 and everyone stayed in.

His next card was a five. Possible straight. The miner caught a seven giving him a pair and high on the board. He bet ten and everyone stayed in the game. The gambler looked at Johnny and then away. He showed a jack and a queen. The final card around showed Johnny Joe with a pair of aces. He missed his straight which would beat three of a kind and two pair.

The other hands showed nothing on top except the pair of sevens so Johnny Joe was high. He bet $50. Everyone but the man with the pair of sevens threw in his cards at once. The miner hesitated, looked at his hole cards again, then shrugged and threw them in.

Johnny knew the kid had another seven in the hole. He would have won but wouldn't risk it. That's why they call it poker and the hand told him a lot about how the miner would play.

The game settled down then. After the first two hours, Johnny was about $600 ahead. The small gambler was over $1,000 ahead. The miner and the oldest man had run out of funds, stood, and walked out without a word. That was poker.

The gambler dealt out the four hands. He

named the game as straight draw poker and just after the last cards hit the table, Johnny Joe stood up.

"Cashier, card count!" Johnny Joe barked. The words whipped through the room like a scythe. In some gambling halls and saloons those words are 'get ready to fight' words, but the cashier had plainly said a card count could be called for.

"Hands on the table!" Johnny Joe snapped, sitting down and pushing his hands out on the table. The other three men did the same.

The cashier came quickly, checked the five cards each in the four hands, then counted the cards in the deck, being careful not to show the face of any card or to disturb their order. When he finished he frowned, then counted again.

When he ended the count this time, he drew his derringer and scowled at the four men. "We have fifty-five cards in this deck. That's three too many. Somebody is cheating."

"I'll submit to a body search," Johnny Joe said quickly.

"Yeah, me, too," the diamond stick pin man said.

"I've got nothing to hide," the dark gambler said.

They all looked at the young man in his

30's who had seemed to be no threat. He was well ahead for the evening. The stick pin man was almost out of chips.

The cashier turned his derringer toward the young man. "Sir, will you submit to a body search?"

"Hell no! Nothing that says I got to. No rules on the list."

The four men still in the other game had stopped play and watched the drama unfold.

The small gambler sighed. "He doesn't have to submit, but we can search him easily enough. There are three of us and only one of him."

The dealer turned gambler paled a little. He scowled, then he gave a sigh. "Look, I won't admit I did anything wrong. Nobody can prove it. I'll just resign from the game and put all of my chips in the current pot." He looked around anxiously. "That make everyone happy?"

"Probably the two men who just went broke won't be pleased when they find out about it," the small gambler said. He shrugged. "That's fine by me."

The ex-dealer looked at the other two men. Both nodded. He pushed more than $1,300 worth of chips into the pot, stood and carefully walked to the door and down the steps. He was not showing a gun.

"Let's play some poker," Johnny Joe said.

The cashier scooped up all the cards and pocketed them, then broke the seal on a new deck and spread it out for the men to see. Then the five card draw game continued with a new deal. The stick pin man who had been almost broke won the game on a full house, aces over fours. He had drawn three cards. It had been fools' luck. But Johnny Joe knew you couldn't argue with winning.

The gambler grinned and Johnny Joe congratulated the older man. But all the big pot did was delay the inevitable. An hour later the stick pin player bet his last twenty-dollar chip and lost the hand.

The $16,000 that started the game was now divided almost equally between Johnny Joe and the gambler. They used trays the cashier provided and went to the far table that still had three players.

After the first two hands with the new players, Johnny Joe had them checked out.

The small gambler from his table sat directly across from him again. To Johnny Joe's left sat a card counter. He loved to play seven card stud and Johnny Joe could almost hear the kid's mind memorizing the cards down and the odds on who would get what on the next round. He looked about 18 and could be dangerous if he could call every deal or on a one-on-one match.

The next man was a cowboy with his hat on. He was a good player but could not bluff and held little threat. Just a matter of time. He was down about $500 so far.

The fifth man now at the table was a silver king, or trying to be. He had silver decorations on his fancy Western style shirt's pockets, cuffs and collar points. He wore a big silver buckle and had a pocket full of silver dollars he toyed with. He played for the enjoyment of the game, the thrill of the competition. He would not last.

It was just past midnight when the cashier came in and announced a small break. He provided free sandwiches and beer. Nobody drank the beer, well aware of the bladder effects.

After the ten minute break they went back to poker. It was Johnny Joe's deal. He returned to the professional's game, draw poker and called for jacks or better. He caught a pair of aces on the deal but the silver king opened. Everyone kept three cards not telling the dealer much. He discarded three and dealt around the pairs, then three to himself.

The gambler watched him carefully as he dealt. Johnny Joe handed out the cards so slowly there was no chance to bottom deal.

The gambler nodded and looked at his down cards.

The bidding had picked up. The silver king had opened for $50 and now bet $100. The bet was to Johnny who had caught another ace in the three cards. He bumped it up $100 and the bet went around at $200 calling Johnny. He laid down his three aces and the others groaned.

"Card count," the gambler called softly. The men kept their hands up on the table as the cashier counted the played out deck.

"Fifty two cards, exactly the right number, gentlemen. Is there any challenge?"

Everyone looked at the gambler who shrugged. "Just wanted to break up the monotony a little. Charlie, you've got to earn your money since the boss isn't here to give you a bad time." They all laughed except the card counting kid.

He didn't call the game, just automatically dealt out a seven card stud hand foundation and then flipped up the first card on each hand. He had a king high and bet $100. By the time the third face card was up, there was over $2,000 in the pot.

Johnny Joe checked his hole cards again for the tenth time. He had a pair of deuces on the deck and absolutely nothing showing. His last down card had been a trey. He was one card short of a straight and one short on a flush.

The others looked at the card counter. He checked his hole card again and counted out $500. The cowboy folded, so did the gambler.

The silver king shrugged and counted out ten fifty dollar chips, the largest they used. He looked at the chips, then at his own hand showing. He had three parts of a ten high diamond straight flush, the ten, nine and eight of diamonds. Both ends were open. Johnny Joe wished good thoughts for him. The silver king checked his three hole cards and pushed his own stack of $500 into the pot.

"You're called, wiseass," he said.

They looked at Johnny Joe. He tossed in his hand.

The card counting kid giggled, a high, strained laugh and turned over one more ace showing three, then turned over a four of clubs, and the last card up was the fourth ace.

"I'll be damned," the small gambler said.

"Nice hand," the silver king said. Then he turned over a seven of diamonds to add to his straight flush. His next card came up a deuce of clubs. He rubbed the last card on the smooth top of the table and slowly turned it over. It was the jack of diamonds.

A straight flush. One of only two poker hands that will beat four of a kind.

"Now I'll be damned," the card counter said. He slumped in his chair and counted his money. He only had a little over $300 left.

The game moved quickly then. The card counter went broke two hands later and left. The cowboy was the next to belly-up. The gambler lucked into a full house of aces over kings in a game of draw poker. He beat the cowboy's three queens.

The silver king held in only because of the nearly $3,000 pot he had won from the card counter. Now he lost steadily and by two A.M. he was down to his last $20. He shrugged, stood up and flipped the chip into the pot.

"Good game men, I enjoyed it. I'll be back next week. Damn, I like to lose money!"

"How much do you have?" Johnny Joe asked.

The silver king scratched his head. "Damn, don't rightly know. Silver, that damn blue stuff we used to call it. Reckon I'm up to about six or eight million by now. Somebody must keep track, I pay them enough to. Probably stealing me blind. But even so, I can lose a thousand a day for the rest of my life and still not run out. Thanks for the game." He turned and waved at the cashier and walked down the steps.

The small gambler looked at Johnny. "I figured we'd be matched up against each other as soon as I saw who was here tonight. I've got about $7,000, you've got about $5,000. Charlie, I think it's time we use the big chips. Bring out the hundreds and five hundreds."

Chapter TEN

The third evening the Outlaws were in San Francisco, the Professor was feeling so good he talked Willy Boy into going out and finding some ladies of the evening with him.

"But I told Gunner we'd walk around and see the bright lights of the city tonight," Willy Boy said.

"Bring him along. I took him to a whore back in Reno. Did he tell you about it?"

Willy Boy shook his head.

"He was scared out of his skin. Evidently his mother told him he had to be extremely careful of girls because they had 'equipment' he didn't have and it could be easily damaged. All he would tell me was that he didn't damage Susie's equipment."

"I'll have a talk with him," Willy Boy said.

"Let me try first. I got him involved in the first place."

The time to talk to Gunner came just after

the two of them had dinner at a cafe on a street not far from their hotel. They were walking back.

"Gunner, you never did tell me what happened when you went to see Susie. Did she hurt you?"

"No. She didn't hurt me."

"Why did you run out of her room?"

"I told you. I didn't want to hurt her . . . her equipment."

"Did she undress, Gunner?"

"Halfway . . . the top."

"So you saw her breasts. Did that scare you, Gunner?"

"Yes. That's her equipment."

The Professor grinned and walked a ways without comment. "Gunner, that woman was a whore, you know what that is?"

"Bad woman?"

"Not really. Some women do nice things for men, make love to them for money. People call them whores, but they are mostly just like all the other women. Just a little different."

"They have equipment?"

"Yes, just like your mother said, but you won't hurt it, Gunner."

"I won't?"

"No, I promise. What a woman can do for

you is very special, you'll feel great. Do you want to try it again, tonight?"

"You be there?"

"Sure, I'll be right in the next room."

"I . . . I'll be alone with a woman?"

"Yes, it's best that way. Whoever she is, she won't hurt you, and you won't hurt her. It's a natural thing. You should have tried it before now."

"I won't hurt her?"

"No, Gunner, and she'll make you feel better than you ever have before. It won't last long, but it's a wonderful feeling."

"Sure I won't hurt her equipment?"

"Positive. Have I ever lied to you, Gunner?"

"No."

"Good. Will you come with us? Willy Boy is coming too, if it's all right."

"Oh, yes." He frowned. "Willy Boy does this with women, too?"

"Yes. Most men do. It's natural. You'll like it."

Gunner thought about that for a minute. "Even if I don't hurt her equipment, I'll still be able to leave if I want to?"

"Sure, anytime. I'll pay the girl. They charge two dollars, maybe more here."

"We rent them, like a horse?"

"Something like that, Gunner."

They were back at the hotel and found

Willy Boy in his room. They all went down the elevator from the fourth floor. Gunner didn't like the little cage on the elevator at first, but soon he decided it was better than climbing up all the stairs.

They found a small fancy lady parlor four blocks over, just down from the gambling halls, and went in the door. Inside it was nicely decorated, with sweeping velvet drapes on the windows and large, soft chairs. Gunner sat down in one and jumped up quickly when two women came through a draped door and smiled at them.

The Professor went over and talked to the two girls quietly. They both looked at Willy Boy and Gunner and grinned.

"A real honest to god virgin?" one of the girls asked, her eyes wide.

"Yes, and his mother has fed him a lot of crap about hurting a woman's equipment. So it's going to take some time."

"Double, it'll cost you double," the soft blonde said.

"How much is that?"

"Eight dollars."

"Give you six, but you treat him like a treasure. He's not half witted, but he's just a little shy and slow."

"Leave him to me," the girl said and led the Professor over to where Gunner sat.

"Gunner, this is Wanda. She's going to show you all about how to feel good, like we talked about. Remember?"

Gunner stood up at once and the girl's eyes widened as she saw how tall he was.

"My, you are a big man. I'll help you understand and show you what to do Gunner. That's a nice name. Come with me, Gunner, right down the hallway."

The Professor walked partway with them and saw Gunner safely inside the door, then he went back and found four lovely ladies in the parlor from which to choose. Willy Boy had already departed with a big blonde girl.

The Professor was in no hurry. He talked to two of the girls, then picked another one who looked like she was no more than seventeen. She wasn't.

Gunner watched Wanda close the door and he frowned, then saw Wanda turn and smile at him.

They talked. Wanda did the best she could to explain to Gunner what his mother had meant.

"Sometimes little boys hit girls and hurt their breasts. They don't mean to, but it happens. That doesn't hurt us bad. But that was what your mother meant. Would you like to see my breasts, Gunner?"

He turned toward the wall. His neck got red and he couldn't think for a minute. "I . . . I've seen some. Susie's."

"Then you know what they look like and that they aren't easy to hurt. When I make you feel good, Gunner, I'll have to have my clothes off. Did you know that?"

"No."

"Would you mind if I took off my dress?"

Gunner looked back at her. Slowly he shook his head.

"Have you wondered what a girl looks like, without her dress?"

Gunner nodded.

"Well, Gunner, now is your chance to see." She slid out of the dress and put it on the edge of the bed where she sat. Gunner watched her. He looked at her breasts, then down at her crotch.

"You haven't got any . . ."

"No, Gunner. That's part of the equipment different between boys and girls."

She watched him, then stood and moved slowly toward him.

"Gunner, is there anything you want to do? Anything you want me to do for you?"

He shook his head.

"Nothing at all, Gunner?" She stopped in front of him, took his hand and put it on her breast. He pulled it back, looked at her wide eyed, then she put it on her soft bare breast again and he left it there.

"See, Gunner, you aren't hurting my equipment at all. You have equipment, too, Gunner. Will you show me your equipment? It's only fair, I've showed you mine."

He frowned. His hand remained motionless on her breast.

"Come on, Gunner, fair is fair. Unbutton your trousers and show me your equipment. I bet it is really big."

He didn't move.

"Can I open your buttons, Gunner?"

He didn't respond. She moved his hand, bent and began opening the buttons on his pants. Gunner's glance moved from her breasts to her hands, watching them opening his fly. Then her hand slipped inside the opening and Gunner jumped up and backed away.

"No. No. That's not nice!"

"It's all right, Gunner. Here in this room, with just you and me, it's all right."

He frowned and stared at her. "Mother told me never, never, never to let anybody touch me there."

"Damn, good old Mom again."

She moved away from him and sat on the bed. "Look, Gunner, I'm here and I'm waiting if you want to do anything. Otherwise you're just wasting your money and my time. I've had about enough of this education for the sadly neglected."

Gunner frowned. "I don't understand."

"Gunner, I know you don't, but you're not going to understand it this time. Maybe the next time. Now button your pants and go out in the lobby and wait for your friends. They should be along shortly."

Gunner frowned again. "Did I do wrong? You mad at me?"

"No, Gunner, I'm not mad. Mostly, I'm mad at your mother. I'm just a little sad for you. Now button up and get out of here." She slipped on her dress and led Gunner back to the lobby.

Willy Boy was sitting there waiting. He jumped up when he saw Gunner and they hurried out the door.

"Lordy, you should have seen mine, Gunner. A big Swede girl, built like a Holstein heifer and she was eager!"

He looked at Gunner. "Everything go all right?"

Gunner shrugged.

"Did you . . . did everything work out?"

"Wanda got mad at me."

"So I guess you didn't. Oh, damn. Maybe next time."

They walked halfway down the block and came back to the brothel.

"Where's the Professor?" Gunner asked.

"He's probably investigating the equipment a little more than we did." Willy Boy looked over at Gunner. "If I was a betting man, I'd say he was investigating it two or three times."

They walked the half block five more tours before the Professor came out. He was grinning at them.

"Sometimes having a shot up arm can gain a great amount of sympathy from certain individuals. A thoroughly and completely enjoyable interlude."

He looked at a poster on a building.

"Well, the opera is on tonight. Would either of you gentlemen care to attend the opera with me?"

"Opera? Is that where the women sing and the men fight with funny little swords?" Willy Boy asked.

"Sing? Sometimes it's pure caterwauling, but they call it singing, even out here in the wilderness. However, I'm willing to give them a chance. Yes, it's the opera for me. I'll see you fellows back at the hotel, much later tonight."

Willy Boy and Gunner watched the Professor stride down the street as if his arm felt perfectly fine. They retraced their steps to the hotel, then found a small song and dance hall and for fifty cents watched a performance of two jugglers, a man and his trained bear and two comedians who were not funny at all.

Long before it was over, Gunner began to yawn. Willy Boy agreed with him and they slipped out into the San Francisco night. They began to walk back to their hotel when two thugs jumped out of an alley. One had a piece of pipe and the other a long stick of wood.

"No problems, mates. Just hand over your valuables and we won't mess up your good looks none. Stand easy like and hand them over. No sense in you getting beaten with a lead pipe, now is there, mates?"

Gunner lunged at one of them, caught the stick in his hands and broke it in half, then clubbed the medium sized man to the ground where he lay half conscious.

Willy Boy pulled his derringer and shot the larger man in the right shoulder, spinning the pipe from his hand.

A police whistle shrilled down the street. Gunner looked at Willy Boy.

"We should run away?"

"Not at all, Gunner. We've done nothing wrong. These two hooligans assaulted us.

We simply defended ourselves." The man with the shot shoulder tried to get up but Gunner whacked him with the stick and he lay on top of his friend in crime.

Sturdy boots smacked the pavement and a moment later a San Francisco policeman hurried up. He looked at them and then down at the pair of muggers.

"You gents all right?" the policeman asked.

"Yes, indeed, officer. These two mistook us for country bumpkins and tried to relieve us of our valuables."

"Didn't I hear a shot, sir?"

"Indeed, officer. A .45 caliber derringer, over and under. One round remaining. I shot him in the shoulder. My friend here took the club away from the other one and pounded him with it."

Just then another officer arrived with a lantern. He shone the light on the two miscreants.

"Yes, Clancy, we know these two. Rounder and Carson. They won't be bothering the public anymore for a long time."

It took them a half hour to go to the police station and answer the questions while the officers filled out a report. The pair of thieves had been running loose in that neighborhood for a month.

The first policeman who had come to the scene walked them back to their hotel, thanked them again and then said good night.

Upstairs in Willy Boy's room, Gunner laughed. "The police were thanking us for helping them," Gunner said. "Usually they're chasing us. Now they are nice to us."

"Helps when you have money, Gunner. This whole world runs on money. If you don't have any, nobody is your friend. That's why I aim to get all the money I can. Banks, I love banks. But now looking at these gambling halls, I think they must have a lot more money than any bank."

Willy Boy said good night to Gunner and went to bed early, wondering if there was any way that they could rob one of the big casinos — and get away without being killed. He would ask the Professor. They were in the perfect spot to do some research and investigation on the subject.

Tomorrow. He would work on that project tomorrow.

Chapter ELEVEN

The two poker players took a short break by mutual consent. It was nearly three A.M. They had been playing poker nonstop since eight the previous day, seven hours.

Johnny Joe was pleased with his play so far. He had stayed with his kind of game, bet well within himself, charged along with one small run of luck, but knew when to fold.

The only problem was this match paid nothing for second place. It was winner take all. If he didn't beat this man he would go back to the hotel a loser by $1,000 and be no better off than the first man who went broke and dropped out of the contest.

The cashier brought out a new deck of cards, broke the seal, extracted the pasteboards, and the last two players from the original twelve began.

The ante was now $100, since that was the smallest chip on the table. They cut for deal and the other man won. He nodded and dealt a hand of five card draw.

On the first four hands they split, each winning two pots about the same size.

The small dark gambler dealt out another hand of five card draw. Johnny Joe held four diamonds and a club. Should he try to draw to a flush? There were nine more diamonds in the deck. But if he did discard just one card, his opponent would know at once he was trying for a flush or a straight, or possibly drawing to two pair.

They were now playing with no openers required, guts poker some professionals called it. It was a bluffing game all the way. Johnny Joe looked at the placid face across from him but could read nothing.

His one club gave him a pair of queens. Not a bad hand to draw to. He waited to see what the dealer threw away. He discarded two cards.

Johnny Joe knew it was time to push it. He threw the club and asked for one card. The dealer looked up and smiled.

"Already you are changing your game. Well, well, well. You must be getting tired."

"Before this, I have played poker continuously for more than 36 hours. I'm just getting warmed up."

The dealer sent Johnny Joe his one card

face down, then with the deck flat on the table, the dealer slid off his own three cards as Johnny Joe watched.

He pushed the new card under the others without looking at it and slowly worked through his diamonds until he saw the new one. A diamond! He didn't let a flicker of emotion show on his face.

The dealer bet in guts poker at this house. Now the other man stared at Johnny Joe trying to figure what he had drawn to the odds of his hitting what he wanted. At last he shrugged and moved two $100 chips into the pot.

Johnny laid out two chips, then two more.

"Raise you $200."

The master bluffer watched his opponent, picked up no hint, met the bet and raised $200 more.

Johnny Joe hesitated just long enough for his opposition to get a hint of indecision, then he added the two $100 chips and tossed in a gold one for $500.

"Cost you $500 more to stay in the hand," Johnny Joe said with a flat, level voice betraying nothing. There was almost $2,000 in the pot. There would be $2,400 if the bet were called.

Johnny Joe knew the man would call, at

this point he had to. The question was, would he raise?

The dark man showed the first sign of doubt. He folded his cards and looked at the pot, then up at Johnny Joe. When he looked back at his cards, he separated them slowly in his hand and stared at them.

"Call," he said and slid a $500 chip into the pot.

Johnny Joe laid down his hand. "Diamonds, queen high," he said softly.

"Damn! Figured you for two pair bluffing me on a full house."

"I know," Johnny Joe said. He pulled in the pot, then picked up the cards and shuffled.

Two more hands passed before they had another interesting game. Johnny Joe dealt a seven card stud game for some variety. It was the first non-draw game of the one-on-one series. The first card turned up to the small dark man was a king of diamonds.

Johnny Joe laid out a queen of clubs for himself and the other man bet $200.

By the time the third up card was played, the other man showed a pair of kings and a five of clubs. Johnny Joe showed the king and queen and ten of clubs. It was a possible royal flush, the best hand in poker.

He knew what he had in the hole, the ace of clubs and a seven of hearts. All he needed was a jack of clubs for a perfect hand. He breathed slowly as he slid his final dealt card over the other two down cards and picked them up. He pulled the top card off and pushed it to the rear of the three. Again he did it drawing up the card slowly.

It was black! It was a jack! Then he revealed the whole card to his eyes only and saw it was the jack of spades. So close. He looked up at the small man who watched him.

"Get it?" the man asked.

Johnny Joe smiled.

The kings were high on the board and the man pushed in two $500 chips.

"I don't believe you got them," the man said. "Cost you $1,000 to convince me."

Johnny Joe stacked up two $500 chips and then four more as the other man watched with surprise. Then Johnny Joe threw his cards on the table face down and pushed them into the pot.

"You're right, I don't have them." He had wound up without even a pair. His ace high was his best hand.

They played three more hands and Johnny Joe won two of them. He was over $2,000 ahead of when he started the two handed game.

Then the poker got rough.

"A thousand dollar ante," the other man said.

The cashier looked up, but said nothing. The rules were more lax on the final man-to-man confrontations.

It was guts poker again with the small man dealing. Johnny Joe waited until all his cards were dealt, then picked them up. He had three jacks. Usually that would be a good enough hand to beat one other man in draw poker. He usually would throw two cards and try for a fourth jack, but that was a low odds bet. Now he saved the ace and discarded one card face down.

"One," he said.

The dealer looked up and smiled. "Trying it again. Damn, twice in a row."

He dealt the card and tried to read his opponent's expression as he looked at the card.

For Johnny Joe it was easy to remain unemotional about the hand. He had bluffed a one card draw and it worked. Now the betting and bluffing were essential. He glanced at the card and to his surprise found another ace. Full house! That beat everything up to four of a kind. There were only three hands that could beat it.

The dealer bet $200. Johnny Joe matched it then bet $1,000.

The other man looked at his cards, snorted. "Trying to bluff me out, right? Not a chance."

He matched the $1,000 and added another $1,000.

It was up to Johnny Joe. He looked at his hand, the full house was still there. He set out two $500 chips and then a $100.

"Your thousand and a hundred just to let you lose some more money if you really want to."

The man checked his cards, then shook his head. "Not a chance you're getting away from me this time." He pushed out a $100 chip and then bet $2,000 more and Johnny Joe considered the wager. It was by far the biggest pot of the whole evening. There would be over $10,000 in the pot if he called. If he did and lost, he would have less than $1,000 left.

"Two thousand to me, correct?" Johnny Joe said. The cashier had lifted from where he had been half asleep and now watched the game.

"Right. How does that four legged straight look now, big spender?"

It was the first real taunt of the evening. Nerves were starting to fray.

"It looks rather good." Johnny Joe pushed in another four of the $500 chips.

"I call, let's see your straight," Johnny Joe said.

It wasn't a straight, but a heart flush that the gambler laid down, a ten high heart flush.

"Not a bad hand," Johnny Joe said. "With those cards I would have bet about the same way you did."

The other man reached for the pot.

"Hold on. Take a look at this." Johnny Joe laid down his full house and the other man sagged in disappointment.

"Damn! I swore you were going for a straight or a flush, missed it, and then wound up bluffing."

Johnny Joe pulled in the chips. He saw that the small man was down to less than $1,000.

On the next three games, Johnny Joe won all three. The other player had only $500 in chips.

The small man dealt a game of guts draw. He put in his ante of $100 and had only $400 left. After they drew cards he checked the bet.

Johnny Joe bet $300 to keep the other man in the game. A quick look of thanks came from the small gambler. He put in his whole $400.

"Three hundred and raise you a hundred," he said softly, not really thinking he could win it now.

Johnny Joe looked at his cards, and pushed in the last chip. He had a pair of queens. "I'll call, what do you have?"

There was no animation on the other man's face now as he glanced at his opponent. He had given up.

The gambler laid out his hand. He had a pair of jacks and no support.

Johnny Joe spread out his queens and the small man stood, reached across the table and shook Johnny Joe's hand.

"A good poker player who gets lucky is impossible to beat," the man said. "A pleasure to meet you, but not to play poker against you. Let me know when you're playing this game, I'll sit out that night. Oh, my name is Flynn Parkinson."

"Johnny Joe Williams. Good to play with a man who knows how to use the cards."

The cashier came and patiently stacked the chips back in the fancy box, and then counted out $12,000 in cash to Johnny Joe.

Parkinson looked at the gold coins a minute, shrugged, and walked down the steps.

When the gold coins were counted, Johnny Joe glanced at the cashier. "I understand you have a bank here on the premises, a kind of company bank."

"Yes sir, we do. We've never lost a dollar of our players' money. It's a vault where we store the money."

"Could you deposit this in my name? I don't want to carry around all that gold."

"I can, sir. Please come downstairs with me so we can find a guard."

Ten minutes later, Johnny Joe had a receipt for $12,000 on deposit in the El Dorado safe. He would get back the same gold he put in. The box had his name on it. He took $200 from his pocket and gave it to the cashier.

"This is for your trouble tonight, and the businesslike way you handled that cheater. Do you catch a player trying to cheat in this game often?"

"He's the first one who has actually been cheating in two months now. We have an excellent reputation."

"He had a sleeve hold out that wasn't very smooth. I could see his coat sleeve move every time he worked it. He must be a beginner at cheating."

"I'll have to be more observant the next time. Thank you for stopping him."

Johnny Joe nodded. "Oh, I'm interested in the big game this weekend. Do you know if it's still planned?"

"Without question. Saturday night at eight. Since you have won a nightly game, you are automatically included among those who are asked to play. I now invite you."

"Good. Now I think I'll find someplace open and have some breakfast, then get a good day's sleep."

"Will you play again tonight, Mr. Williams?"

"No, I'm afraid I would go to sleep over my cards. As soon as I'm rested properly, I'll be back. Saturday night, yes, I'm looking forward to that."

Johnny Joe turned and walked out of the now strangely silent and dark casino accompanied by an armed guard. Johnny Joe pressed the derringer in his jacket pocket to be sure the .45 caliber weapon was there.

On the street a one horse hack waited. One of the guards said a big winner was still inside who would be coming out shortly.

Johnny Joe jumped in the hack and gave the hotel's address and leaned back. A moment later the rig turned into a side street and stopped suddenly. Two men jumped on the buggy, one in each door. One of them had a six-gun.

"Big winner, where's the gold?" the man with the gun demanded.

"Right here," Johnny Joe said. He had

taken out his .45 derringer when he got in the coach and held it on the seat beside his leg. Now he turned his hand only slightly in the darkness of the hack and fired. The round hit the gunman in the side of the head and jolted him off the buggy, killing him before he hit the cobblestones.

The driver screeched at the horse and the rig raced down the street a block. Then the driver jumped down and ran into the darkness.

Johnny Joe slid out of the buggy and walked the rest of the way to the hotel in the black San Francisco night as a thick fog began to thin. He still had one shot in his derringer. Johnny Joe decided against breakfast.

It was after five A.M. before he at last locked the door in the hotel and slid onto his bed.

He was $12,000 richer! He wouldn't have to touch the money from the payroll robbery. It would be divided among the members of the Outlaws.

Johnny Joe smiled as he began to get sleepy. He had paid his dues, he had gained admittance to the BIG GAME. Now all he had to do was win it. That was all.

Johnny Joe slept.

Chapter TWELVE

Deputy Sheriff Seth Andrews got off the stage in Virginia City knowing what he would discover, but he had to do it anyway. It might give him some indications where the bastards were heading next.

Deputy Andrews was from Oak Park, Texas, and had an ugly scar on his head where Willy Boy Lambier had shot him. The bullet had only grazed his scalp, taking out a thin line of skin, but it had numbed his brain for a day and the powder burns turned him nearly bald for a month and left an ugly scar.

Now his hair had grown over most of the wound but he still had headaches. He still had the nightmares as well, reliving time and time again how he ran into the cell block and found Willy Boy Lambier had hanged himself from the top bunk. The kid's face was blue, his eyes rolled back in his head and his tongue lolling out.

Seth had to cut him down fast!

He ordered the big guy, Gunner, to stand back in the two man cell so he could rush in and lift the kid off the bunk to relieve the pressure on his windpipe.

That was when the bastard grabbed the deputy's six-gun and tried to kill him with a shot in the head. Thank god he almost missed. Blood? Blood everywhere when he finally woke up. But he couldn't even get to the front door to call for help.

The sheriff found him the next morning half dead, bleeding like a stuck shoat.

"Goddamn your black heart, Willy Boy!" Deputy Seth Andrews said. "I'm gonna get your ass yet and when I do I won't never bring you back for trial. No sireeee Bub!"

He had trailed them to Kansas and then on into Idaho, but they were too tough to pin down. He got wind of them heading for the railroad and he followed.

But he was way too late to stop them from robbing the bank at Winnemucca, Nevada. It had to be them. Same methods, six men. Then he figured they had taken the train and his best guess was that they had gone west. He didn't know why, but when he got a report on the telegraph about six men robbing a mine payroll in Virginia City, Nevada, he knew he had found their trail again.

He'd get them eventually.

It took him a half a day of interviewing the mine men involved and the local deputy sheriff to be sure it was Willy Boy. The giant and the Indian and the Mex made a combination that was hard to hide. He had found them again. The sheriff of Storey County where the mine was, seemed to be in a hospital somewhere recovering. They didn't exactly say from what.

It had taken Seth a half day in Virginia City and now he was anxious to get moving. The stage didn't leave until the morning, they said. A change in schedule. He'd take the Central Pacific.

The ticket agent had been snotty. Said of course he had sold six tickets to Sacramento about a week ago. He sold batches of six and eight tickets every day. No, he didn't remember what the men looked like who bought them.

The Professor could be a gambler, maybe one or two more of them. Johnny Joe was a gambler too, according to his notes. Yes, nobody would get this close to San Francisco and not go there. Part of it was that he wanted to go there himself. He'd heard about San Francisco ever since he was big enough to read.

Once in the big city, he had gone straight to the Chief of Police. He spread out his warrants and detailed some of the crimes the men had committed.

The San Francisco Police Chief was a tall man evidently appointed for his political connections, not his lawman qualifications.

"Deputy Andrews. I will be more than pleased to honor your warrants and assist in any way that I can if you find these six men. However . . ." he held his arms out, palms up. "Six out of a city of what soon will be a hundred and fifty thousand? You have taken on for yourself an impossible job."

"It hasn't been easy since I started, Chief. And you certainly are right, it ain't got any easier as it goes on. But I got me a blood oath to find these killers."

"You say you think one or two of them are gamblers. You could frequent the several gambling halls in our city. At one time we had over a thousand, but I'd say now you shouldn't have to cover more than about two hundred. The larger ones would be the establishments they would go to, which cuts it down even farther to something like a dozen."

"Where might I find these establishments?"

"Goodness sakes, how long have you been in town? Simply walk around Portsmouth Square and you'll be able to see most of them. Now, if you have no more questions . . ."

Seth found himself back on the street, asking where to find this Portsmouth Square. He found it and at first went into the Bella Union. It was a huge gambling hall with all sorts of games of chance. At one time he fancied himself a pretty good poker player, but he knew he didn't have the stake it would take to get serious in a game here.

He walked around the tables, with his lawman's critical eye watching for Johnny Joe Williams. After an hour in the Bella Union, and a beer and some free sandwiches from the bar, he had to admit that he hadn't spotted Williams and there was an overwhelming chance that he never would.

Even if Williams were in this gambling emporium, Seth could pass within a foot of him in this crush and never even see him.

At the far end of the hall he found a small stage and he mounted four steps and stood there looking over the assembly. No one was performing but he saw advertisement posters indicating that there would be a show every three hours.

For an hour he stood there watching the constant parade of humankind that worked up and down the floor, often from one table and game of chance to another. He saw no one that even resembled any of the Willy Boy Gang.

Seth left the Bella Union and went outside. Nearby, the El Dorado advertised the prettiest barmaids in town. He went in, bought a beer from one of the small and attractive girls, ate two of the larger sandwiches and walked the big hall watching for the Willy Boy Gang members. He saw none of them.

He heard something about a big game going on upstairs. He asked one of the men about it.

"Poker. Big game. You buy $1,000 worth of chips and then play upstairs somewhere. Don't even get up there without the chips. Then everyone plays until one man has all the money. Sometimes they get twenty, twenty-five players."

"And one man winds up with $20,000 to $25,000?"

"Dern tootin'! Just wish it was me."

He asked where the stairs were and went there but when he approached the man who guarded it, he was asked if he had the $1,000 buy in fee.

"No, I'm afraid not, I'm a lawman and I just . . ."

"You're not from around here, lawman, so you don't count. You go see San Francisco lawmen you want something done here."

"I just wanted to watch."

"Nobody watches, not even the owners or the men who lose all of their money. Now move along, the game is just starting and the door above is closed."

Deputy Sheriff Seth Andrews wandered out of the El Dorado and looked at the other now brightly lighted gambling halls. He hadn't even realized that it had grown dark. He asked a passerby where a good hotel was, then he amended that to a medium priced hotel and was directed to one several blocks away.

He would register there and get a good night's sleep, then be fresh in the morning to find some other avenue of locating the six men he searched for.

The first day he had been in San Francisco, Juan Romero found the part of town where the Mexicans lived. It was far at the edge, down along the bay, but the houses were substantial and the cafe was pleasant and he had felt at home again. He ate of dishes of old Mexico and dreamed of his Juanita and his baby boy Ernesto.

Once he cried and the friendly barman gave him another tequila. He remembered something about the offer of a bed for the night and he knew he had drunk too much to try to get back to his hotel.

The next morning he woke up with Conchita sleeping soundly beside him. Both of them were naked.

She awoke when he moved and she whispered something in Spanish to him and he shook his head, trying to clear the fog of too much liquor from his brain.

Then Conchita sat on his stomach and urged him to do what he had done so wonderfully last night.

"Just one more time," she said.

Juan pushed her away and dressed as quickly as he could. The cafe was open and he asked for some coffee.

"You made Conchita happy last night," the big barman said. "She likes you."

Juan asked how much he owed for the bed and liquor, paid it gladly and slipped out the door before Conchita got to the cafe.

Now he was going back to see if Conchita was still there. A man had needs, and he had not been with a woman since he left his Juanita near Brownsville.

Today he would tell Conchita that he was married and that he was going home soon. She would understand.

He tried to tell her, but Conchita grabbed him and hurried him to her bedroom and before he knew it they were making love again.

Later as she combed her long black hair he found the courage to tell her. She threw down the comb and picked up a pair of scissors and tried to stab him.

He leaped away.

"No, Conchita. Do not do this. I am your friend."

"You are my lover, not my friend. I thought you would marry me. Now you say that you're already married." She lunged at him again and snagged his shirt and tore it. He jumped over the bed and watched her.

"I tried to tell you."

"You tried to seduce me."

"It wasn't a difficult job."

"I will kill you. My father will kill you. My five brothers will hang you by your balls and then they will kill you."

Juan knocked the scissors from her hand and grabbed her. He made her sit on the bed and he put his arms around her. She was still naked and crying softly.

"I did not mean to make love to you the first night. You got me very drunk. You were drunk too, no? It was an accident. I am sorry."

"I'm pregnant. I know I have your baby. It is the right time. I feel pregnant."

"Sometimes you remind me of my Juanita when you look like that. She is so beautiful, like you. We have a small son, Ernesto. He would like you. You have much bigger tetas than my Juanita. You are more slender, more beautiful."

"Then stay here with me, marry me and I will give you a dozen fine sons!"

"I'm already married."

"We can pretend to be married. No one will know."

"God will know."

"He will not care if we are happy."

"I can't do that. It would be a sin. No man can have two wives."

Conchita dressed quickly and before he thought to stop her she ran out. He finished dressing and hurried after her. She went into the cafe and the man behind the counter was waiting for Juan. He had a meat cleaver and the cutting edge shone with its sharpness.

"Bastard!" the bar man shouted. "You have ruined my jewel, my Conchita. You tease her with your money and then you take her virginity."

"Conchita was not a virgin, probably not for five years has she known what a virgin feels like," Juan said. He adjusted the six-gun on his thigh and the big man behind the counter calmed down.

"I was wrong. I was drunk. But you fed me the tequila, and you brought Conchita to my table. You are as to blame as I am. My friend, since you are Mexican, I will do you a favor. I will not shoot you between the eyes for tricking me. I will not burn down your cantina for being mean to me. And I will not report you to the authorities for running a house of prostitution without a license.

"What I will do is turn and walk away, and hope that you are more kind to strangers in the future." From his pocket he took a twenty dollar gold piece and flipped it to the woman he figured was only about twenty years old.

"Conchita, you are a whore, you should be paid like a whore. Go enjoy the money, buy yourself a new dress and a new blouse. Just be sure your papa here doesn't get any part of the gold."

Juan turned and walked away, curiously wondering more about what the girl would do than her father. He had been set up to be seduced and then forced into a marriage. It was the last time he would admit that he had more than a few pesos in his pocket. Quickly he checked his purse, but it was safely deep in his pocket.

He walked up the street to the far end of the Mexican settlement, eased into a small cafe and ordered some refried beans and some enchiladas. He ate with relish, had a glass of strong Mexican beer and walked back to the hotel in the middle of San Francisco feeling much better.

Soon he would return to Mexico. He had decided that they would probably go back to Denver and try the bank with the Professor, then it would be his turn to go to Mexico. If the group did not go, he would simply slip away. He would have paid his debt to Willy Boy by that time.

That afternoon he sent three letters to his Juanita in care of his uncle who lived near the border. In each one he put a fifty dollar bill and a letter telling Juanita how much he missed her and Ernesto.

Soon it would be the day he went home to them. With the money he had, and had sent home, his family could live like a king in Mexico.

Chapter THIRTEEN

Francis X. Delany sat in his private office in the El Dorado and looked down on the floor through a small window. Few people knew of his office or that he could see the whole floor. It had come in handy often.

He took a long pull from a glass of lemonade and turned back to his desk. Five years ago the doctors told him to stop drinking alcohol. That almost killed him. Now, at 61, he had learned to live with the minor inconveniences.

Delany was a roundish man, with thinning gray hair, small liver spots developing on the backs of his hands and his left cheek, and a short body. He weighed 50 pounds too much but couldn't seem to get rid of the weight.

He had a reddish complexion that had been aggravated by his heavy drinking, but now the color remained for no good reason. His nose was a roundish bulb with hairs extending from the nostrils and a pimple on the right side. His eyes were soft blue but now with a hint of growing whiteness on one that bothered him. As long as he could read his poker cards he wouldn't worry about it.

His hands were long with thin fingers and meticulously manicured fingernails. A young lady did them for him each day and also cut his hair and tended to any other physical needs that he might have.

Lately he had insisted that she not do his manicure in the nude, and that he would bed her not more than once a week. At 61 he was starting to find that intense sexual activity wore him out for the whole day.

Delany was a rich man, he had done well. Perhaps now was the time to walk away from it. Sell out his gambling palace and retire to a big house on the hill and take a trip to New York and on to Paris and London. He understood they had some outstanding gambling halls in London, private clubs they were called.

No. No, not yet. He was still a gambler. He had gambled on everything but his own life. That was not a matter for chance. Now his Saturday night games gave him the biggest thrill. The glory of the chase. The thrill of the hunt. He had it all when he was sitting in the room with the best gamblers around, pitting his skill against them, against all of them. And then to come down to the final two men, betting their wits and cards and sometimes their tricks to win $100,000, or $200,000.

This week they had 23 firm reservations for the game. Twenty-three men who would gamble $15,000 each that they could out-play, outlast and out hustle the best poker players in San Francisco for the chance to take home $345,000. It would be the biggest game ever. The most money on the line.

He had to win it. Twice before he had sat in on the biggest game. Once he won. The next time he lost just to set up this monster game.

Saturday night was the night.

He would win . . . one way or the other. If he had to assist Lady Luck, it would be done so delicately that no one would even suspect, let alone be able to call him on it or prove it.

Finesse. Everything had to be done smoothly, stylishly, and so well executed that there was no chance for failure. The call for a simple card count had long since failed to bother him. When you add one you take one away. So simple most card players missed the point entirely.

Subtle, effective, undetectable.

Delany lit a long brown cigar and blew

smoke at the ceiling. He would win the monstrously large pot. There was a chance for $375,000, if two more men signed up. They had a limit of 25 on the game but it had never been reached. Perhaps Saturday night.

Delany looked up as someone knocked on his door.

"Come in," he called and the door opened. A thin, tall man with blond hair lunged into the room. Behind him, pushing, was one of his floor guards.

"This is the man, Mr. Delany," the guard said. The enforcer held a .45 six-gun aimed at the thin man who had his wrists tied together in front of him.

Delany looked at a paper on his desk. "Wolpert, is that your name?"

"Yes sir."

"You were a black jack dealer?"

"Yes sir."

"Until you were caught cheating. Your confederate got away, I understand. Exactly how much did you cheat me out of, Mr. Wolpert?"

"Not much, sir. I've offered to make full repayment. I have employment in another casino."

"You won't work in any other casino in town worthy of the name after I tell them about you, Mr. Wolpert. Is that clear? You will have to leave San Francisco if you want to work in a gambling hall again."

Another man appeared at the door. He carried a six-by-six timber three foot long. He sat it on the floor beside the desk and came back a moment later with a foot long cardboard box which was closed. He laid it on the desk. Two more men came in the room. Both were large, sturdy, unsmiling.

"You are right handed, Mr. Wolpert?"

"Yes sir."

"You admit that you cheated, allowing a gambler at your table to win by bottom dealing, then paying off on his winning bets."

"I told you that before. I figure I owe you maybe $600, no more. I can have the money for you this afternoon."

"That will be too late, Mr. Wolpert."

"Why?"

"You will now receive your punishment, Mr. Wolpert."

The two big men moved quickly beside Wolpert, forced him to his knees beside the six-by-six timber. One of the men cut the bindings that held his hands together. Then he caught Wolpert's right hand, closed the fingers into a fist and taped Wolpert's fingers and thumb together. When they finished they had left Wolpert's first finger extended and the rest closed and taped together tightly.

"Nooooooooooooooooooo," Wolpert wailed. "You can't do this! I've heard about it, but I figured it was just talk. You can't! I earn my living with my hands!"

He tried to lunge away but one of the big men slapped him hard along the side of his head and he swayed against the other large person holding him. Wolpert shook his head and looked down at the squared off end of the heavy timber. There were deep reddish black stains on it, and indentations as if they had been made by an axe.

"Dear God, No!" he screamed. One of the big men put a gag around his head and through his open mouth so his screams came out only as faint, gurgling complaints.

Delany took the top off the cardboard box and lifted out a ten-inch meat cleaver with a five-inch-wide blade that had been filed and honed into razor sharpness. He hefted the tool, which had been fitted with a leather sheath around the handle.

"Let's do it, gentlemen. I've wasted too much time on this matter already. You know what to do with him."

One of the men lifted Wolpert's right hand and pushed it hard against the side of the timber so his finger extended flat on top of it.

"Steady," Delany said. He lifted the cleaver. Wolpert roared through the gag and dove forward, knocking over the six-by-six and dragging the larger guards with him.

"Do it right!" Delany bellowed. The guards took turns and each slammed his fist into Wolpert's face, then dragged him to his knees and set up the block again. This time when they forced his hand against the six-by-six, they were braced so the smaller man could not lunge in any unprotected direction. The finger quivered on the block, moved slightly upward.

Delany raised the cleaver and before anything else could happen, slammed the wide axe downward, severing Wolpert's first finger between the end joint and the middle knuckle. Wolpert fainted.

One of the men grabbed the bleeding stump with a thick cloth and the other lifted the unconscious man and they carried him outside. Another man took out the box, the cleaver and the six-by-six.

Delany looked up as a foppish young man came in. He wore a yellow shirt and a brown jacket and suede shoes.

"Again?" he asked. "Another finger?"

"Yes, whisper it around. Nothing official,

but I want every dealer I pay to know damn well that it could happen to them. I want them to believe it. I won't tolerate cheating on my floor."

"Of course." The young man hesitated. "Oh, Charlie tells me that the Saturday night dance card is filled. We'll have twenty-five players in the big game. Congratulations, sir."

"Well done. Tell Charles there will be a bonus for him. I repay my employees who do good work."

When the foppish young man had left, Delany stood and moved toward the door. He went along a hallway, through a locked door and into the upstairs gaming room where he would play Saturday night.

He did reserve one chair for himself. No one sat there except him and the spot had a few special advantages. A man with a telescope thirty feet away behind the wall could watch the hand of the man directly across from Delany. That part had been easy, but how to communicate what he held to Delany had been the problem. They tried hand signals, but then Delany himself banned any watchers at the game.

He rigged a small bell that could be rung so many times, once for two pair, twice for three of a kind. But everyone could hear it and would soon figure out the reason it rang.

There had to be a better way.

It was weeks before he figured it out. The system could be used only in critical situations. The telescope was behind the enemy player, the solution must be behind him as well. A window was put in the far wall that looked out over the roof. It was two feet square and showed little view. It was four feet from where the telescope man sat in a small walkway next to the outer wall.

The system worked with visual signs that the opponent couldn't see behind him. One red stick held in the window meant the other man had two pair. Two red sticks meant he had three of a kind. For a straight it was one yellow stick and two yellow for a flush.

If the enemy man had a full house a black stick was shown. Two black sticks was for four of a kind and three black sticks for a straight flush.

It was amazing how well the system worked. It gave Delany the ability to bet up when he was a proved winner, or to drop out when he knew he was beaten.

He didn't always use the system. Once in a while he would bet up when he knew he would lose. That would bolster the confidence of the man he was cheating.

He had used the system twice in the past two weeks on smaller games, and both times it had worked well. The system would work in the daytime or at night, since the room was extremely well lighted with half a dozen chandeliers holding four lamps each.

The window in the far wall was illuminated as well so the sticks could be seen against the lighter background.

Now he double checked the system, talked to the man who used the telescope and held up the sticks. He decided that nothing needed to be changed.

Downstairs he paced around the casino floor, talking to a big bettor here, joking with a man in a top hat. He shook the hand of a man wearing miner's pants and boots and a plaid shirt and slouch hat. The man looked much the way he had the first time Delany saw him three years ago.

That night the miner had lost his poke of gold dust quickly and headed back to the mines. The next time he came down a year later, he was worth over a million dollars. Now he was three times that rich, but he still wore his mining clothes and was proud of them.

Delany watched the betting at the roulette wheel. He could never understand men's fascination with the wheel and the bouncing little ball. The odds were alarmingly for the house.

He saw one miner who had a poke of gold dust on the table. Rather than weigh out an ounce of gold for each buying of chips, the dealer put a red chip on the poke whenever the miner lost his bet, and a white one on it whenever he won. When the gambler reached the limit of red chips, his poke was put under the table and he was out of the game. If he won, the white chips were at once cashed in for gold coins by the dealer.

Gold coins were the medium of exchange in all the gambling houses. Few accepted paper money and when they did it was heavily discounted, up to forty percent in some cases. Hard case gamblers hoarded their gold coins for gambling, and big casinos were forced to buy coins wherever they could.

Delany worked along the tables. Faro was still king of the hall. He had more tables for faro than any other game. Roulette, rondo, *rouge et noir* and *vingt-et-un* were also popular. Poker was becoming more popular and a few casinos used the southern game that the blacks had popularized called dice or craps. He wouldn't let it inside his place. It was undignified and since few gamblers asked for it anyway, he let them play the more popular games.

The gamblers still went for the quick game. That, he decided, was why faro and the roulette wheel were so popular. A grown working man could lose his entire month's paycheck in just a few minutes gambling on either table.

Delany talked to a few more people, saw that his barmaids were doing a good business, and went back up the stairs to his office.

He looked at his nails. Yes, he did need a manicure today. Perhaps this would be the time when he would encourage the small, sweet Lucinda to do his nails in the nude. He felt an old urge coming on, and hurried out to call the girl to come in with her tools, and her special talents. It was going to be a good day.

Not once since the cheating dealer left his office had Delany thought about the man. His people had taken him to the casino doctor who worked special gambling privileges.

Yes, it was going to be a good day — but he felt like a little kid, just knowing that he couldn't wait until Saturday and the big game.

He thought of the total and smiled.

"Three-hundred and seventy-five thousand dollars," he said softly.

That was when Lucinda came in and began to peel out of her clothes. She was small and dark with hand sized breasts and a saucy little smile that fascinated him. He wasn't sure if she was sixteen or seventeen, but he didn't care. She was efficient and knew exactly what to do to pleasure him.

Chapter FOURTEEN

It was Friday morning and all of the Outlaws but Johnny Joe were in Willy Boy's room in the hotel. Willy Boy paced the room for a minute, then looked at them.

"Pretty nice here, right? Good food, nice soft bed, games, girls, whatever you want. Only problem is I'm getting restless. Johnny Joe tells me each of these big gambling halls has its own bank. That's where Johnny Joe left his $12,000 he won night before last.

"Our gambling friend is out making contacts and doing his business. Seems like we should get on with some of ours. Professor, I been thinking about knocking over one of those gambling hall banks. They have safes but, hell, you told me that with a few sticks of dynamite you could blow the door off any safe made."

The Professor looked up from where he was dealing himself a hand of solitaire.

"Sure, true, but don't these places have

tons of security around their vaults?"

"Some, but nothing a few sawed off shotgun blasts won't take care of damn quick," Willy Boy said.

"True, but one of the gambling halls where I went made me check my six-gun at the door."

"They all do that. They don't like hideouts much but we know there are lots of them around. The important thing is that Johnny Joe said some of those safes could have $200,000 in them on a good night."

"Two hundred . . . that's more than any bank I've ever seen," the Professor said. "Damn! Two hundred thousand! Are you sure about that?"

"What Johnny Joe said. He should know."

"Hell, Professor, with your share you could open your own college somewhere," Eagle said.

They all laughed.

"Johnny Joe said these big houses get used to having a lot of money around. They need it in case some lucky roulette wheel player hits it big. What do all of you think? Should we take a look into this situation, do some scouting around, maybe get back into business here?"

Everyone there voted yes.

Willy Boy's brown eyes sparkled. He ran

his hand through his hair and grinned. "Good! Yeah, damn good. Now all we have to do is figure out which one of the big ones would be easiest. The Professor and I will work on that part.

"Eagle, you find out where we can buy six good horses and saddles.

"Juan, you and Gunner check out a spot and buy us some trail gear, blankets, cooking things, and food for say a week. I figure the lawmen will be watching the ferryboat to Oakland after we hit the gambling hall. Our best route will be down south on the peninsula here and around the end of the big bay. Then we can work back north and get to Sacramento to jump the train. We can take a week or so and by then nobody will be looking for us."

The Professor nodded. "Yes, I agree. That would be our best avenue of retreat and escape."

Eagle looked at Juan. "Hey, what the hell did the Professor just say?"

They all laughed.

That afternoon, the Professor and Willy Boy quickly discovered what they had suspected. There was no real chance to find out anything about the safes in the gambling halls. They wanted to know where the lock boxes were situated, what kind of locks and designs they had, and what security was kept around them day and night. All those facts were deep dark secrets.

The only reason Johnny Joe got to look at the safe in the El Dorado was because it was the middle of the night and he was helping to carry the gold.

"Hell," the Professor said as they stood at the bar having a beer in the Parker House. "We're not learning much."

In addition to the Parker House, they had been to the Bella Union, Mazourka, Arcade, Varsouvienne, Dennison's Exchange, La Souciedad, Verandah, Empire, Fontine House, Alhambra and the Meade. These were twelve of the most prosperous big time gambling halls in town. All were overflowing with bettors and armed guards. At night, when most of them closed down after one A.M., there probably were additional guards.

"We'll ask Johnny Joe," Willy Boy said. "Right now it looks like we just pick out one and charge in with shotguns blasting and see what we can find."

"Where do we buy the dynamite?"

"Almost any hardware store. I'll put on my trail clothes and go get some later today. How much do you need?"

They settled on ten sticks, enough for two

good sized blasts, and detonators and burning fuse.

"Get a dozen caps and extra fuse," the Professor said. "Then if we have to we can use half sticks of the dynamite like small hand thrown bombs if we get chased."

They left the gambling hall and walked slowly back to the hotel.

"Tonight's the night for Gunner," the Professor said. "I had a long talk with him the other day. He's interested in girls, but his damn mother put the fear of hell in him. He thought if he touched a girl's hand he could make her pregnant. Took me two hours but I explained a lot of things to him and now I think he's ready to lose his virginity."

"Damn, Professor. Why didn't you have your fatherly talk with me?"

They chuckled and continued back to the hotel.

Once Willy Boy changed into his trail clothes, he walked around until he found a hardware store that sold dynamite. The clerk had the "new fangled dynamite sticks," and explained carefully to Willy Boy how to use the powder, the detonators and the fuse.

"Just be careful to carry the detonators and the dynamite separate," the clerk said.

"Then if something sets off the more sensitive detonators, it won't blow you sky high when the dynamite goes off."

Willy Boy nodded.

"You see, the burning fuse sets off a charge in the detonator and that charge explodes the dynamite. We call that a sympathetic explosion. You tape the sticks of powder together and when one goes off it sets off the next one to it until all two or three or four go off at once so quick you think it's one big bang."

"That's what I need on them danged rocks. Want to turn them into little pieces so I can get my foundation set."

The clerk nodded. He bundled up the ten detonators in a padded box so they wouldn't touch one another, and put in the ten feet of burning fuse.

"Remember, the fuse is supposed to burn a foot a minute, but it depends. I had some the other day that burned nearly two feet in a minute, so be careful of it."

Willy Boy paid for the goods and left the store before he got his other arm talked off. He didn't have to know about dynamite. That was the Professor's specialty. He did carry the package with great care all the way back to the hotel room and then put it down gently under the bed.

Just thinking about robbing one of the big casinos gave him goose bumps. It would be the biggest strike of his life. He had to make it good, absolutely perfect. He'd ask Johnny Joe to help them pick out the best place to rob. He hoped for a good sized amount of money, an easy getaway out a back or side door, and some way to confuse anyone who tried to chase them. Willy Boy grinned. He had a good feeling about this one, like it was going to turn out better than any of them expected.

Eagle at last found a livery stable. There were lots of horses in San Francisco, but the stables all seemed to be private or well on the outskirts of the town itself.

At last he hailed a hack and told the driver to take him to the nearest livery barn where he could rent or buy a riding horse. The driver had to think a minute, then drove him over two miles to a place along the bay that had a good sized stable.

The man who ran it spit tobacco juice and squinted as he looked at Eagle.

"Comanche, I'd bet a button," the older man said. "Seen a bunch of you in Texas. You folks all civilized yet?"

"No sir, and I've come to take your scalp," Eagle said with a grin.

The Texan laughed. "About the size of it,

young feller. Me, I never had any trouble with your people, but then I stayed pretty much to the town I lived in. The settlers out on the frontier was the ones who had the troubles. What can I do for you?"

"Two friends and me are riding down to Los Angeles, end of the week. We'll need three good riding horses and saddles. Can you help us?"

"How much you want to pay?"

"Enough so the nags won't drop over before I get them out the front gate."

"You're talking forty, fifty dollars."

"Sounds fair, and ten dollar saddles," Eagle said.

"Maybe less. Let's do some horse buying here."

They went into the lot and Eagle roped a horse he liked. They agreed on $50. The next two he picked out were $40 and $50. He had them put in a stall in the barn and put a big C for Comanche on the end of the three stalls.

The saddles were easier. They wouldn't be riding in them long. He picked out two for $7 apiece and one for $10. He stacked them next to the stall.

"Be a couple of days until my partners take care of some family business," Eagle said. "You keep them fed and watered as usual." He paid the man in gold, eight double eagles and four silver dollars.

Eagle had told the hack driver to wait and now he rode back into town and paid for the drive. He didn't want to buy six horses all at once. One of the others would have to get the other three horses from that or another stable.

Back at the hotel, Eagle knocked on Juan's door and the Mexican opened it up and waved him in. The room looked like a general store. Blankets, boxes of food, and sacks of goods lined the wall.

"We're not going hungry before we get to the train," Juan said and laughed. "I'm getting used to this gringo food, and it isn't bad at all."

That night after supper, the Professor knocked on Gunner's door and grinned when he saw the big man. He had on his town clothes, a white shirt, string tie and a jacket. It was the first time the Professor had seen Gunner in a jacket.

"Hey, you look elegant," the Professor said. "All set to let some pretty little lady take your clothes off?"

Gunner grinned. "I guess. You say I'll like it, so hell, I'll give it a try. You sure I won't hurt her?"

"Not a chance. These girls are used to getting poked. That's how they survive. We rob banks. They get poked. Now, we all ready?"

They went to the same whore house they had before, and the Professor talked to an older woman. She sent for Wanda.

Wanda walked in wearing a yellow robe with her hair on top of her head to make her look taller. She grinned, then lifted her brows when she saw Gunner.

"Oh, yeah, the shy one. You ready to give it another try?"

Gunner nodded. She took his hand. Gunner sent one frantic look toward the Professor, but already he had his arm around a girl and was walking toward another door with her.

"Come on Gunner, got to be a first time. It's nothing after that. You won't think it's such a big deal. Trust me, Gunner, I never lie about sex."

They went down the hall to the same room as before and as soon as they were inside, Wanda pulled off her robe.

"You do have different equipment, don't you?" Gunner said.

"Yes, Gunner. Women have been different from men for a long, long time. Hadn't you noticed?"

"Yes, but I never touched them before. You sure it won't hurt? My mother said to be real careful . . ."

Wanda put her hand on her hip. "Look, your mama isn't here, Gunner. She messed you up enough with her goody-goody talk. Forget all that stuff your mama told you. She told you wrong. Trust me. Let me show you."

Gunner frowned. "You'll show me all of your equipment?"

"Hard not to in my current state of dress. Yes, damnit!"

"Don't get mad at me."

"Gunner, I'm not mad. Let's take off your shirt."

"The Professor didn't say I had to undress."

Wanda shrugged. "You don't, but it makes it a lot easier. Why not take off your shirt?"

Gunner shrugged the way Wanda had and grinned. "Okay."

She began unbuttoning his shirt and he stared at her. At last he smiled. "You're pretty all over . . . naked that way," Gunner said.

"Well, Gunner, we're making some progress. You're pretty, too." Wanda worked on the buttons on Gunner's shirt. She kept talking all the time.

Gunner looked at her. "Do I . . . do I have to take off my pants?"

"Helps, Gunner. I'm naked, don't you think it's only fair that you should be, too? Fair is fair, Gunner. Don't you think that's right?"

Gunner watched her for a minute, stared at her bare breasts and then the thick dark swatch that covered her crotch. At last he shrugged. "I guess."

Wanda grinned but kept on talking. "Did I tell you about my dog? I had this puppy when I was a little girl and one day she got all fat and had puppies. I'd never seen puppies before. Do you like puppies, Gunner? Anyway, they were the cutest little things."

Wanda had his belt unfastened and his pants unbuttoned and still she talked. That's what would do it for Gunner. She sighed and nodded. Now she knew it was only a matter of time.

Chapter FIFTEEN

Johnny Joe slept in late Saturday morning, almost to noon. He was ready. He ate twice in the afternoon, but consumed almost no fluids. By seven-thirty he had performed in the outhouse behind the saloon and walked into the El Dorado.

At the table near the stairway that led to the gaming room overhead, Johnny Joe presented Charlie, the cashier, with his receipt for $12,000 from the El Dorado's safe and nearly ten pounds of double gold eagles in a leather sack. There were 150 coins there filling out his $15,000 entry fee. He signed the receipt over to Charlie, took a special blue paper receipt for his $15,000 fee, and walked up the steps.

Johnny Joe had worn a new white shirt with a ruffled front, and an elaborate tie bunched around his throat and held with a stick pin. His jacket was new, a soft brown weave that had cost him almost $30. It was tailored to fit him.

At noon he had shaved as close as possible, brushed his teeth, and combed his brown hair into a high wave to add a little to his stature.

Now he was ready. He stepped out into the room of high rollers.

No one looked at anyone else. There were no small conversations going on. This was high stakes poker and could make a man's reputation — or send him home broke.

He saw the silver king who had played in the nightly game with Johnny Joe two days ago and lost. He was the only other man Johnny Joe knew in the gathering of eight men. There would be more. He sat down in a chair at one of the tables. He would conserve his strength. He heard there would be 25 players . . . a total of $375,000 at stake! The largest pot ever.

He sucked in his breath. What a treasure! With that kind of money he could buy himself a gambling hall on the square and go into business.

Not to think of that now, it was the game that counted. He would have to play the best poker of his life for at least 24 hours before there would be a chance to go for the big money. It was a case of survival.

As he waited, he examined the room for any possible way that a man could cheat. He saw little. There were no strategically placed mirrors. There would be no visitors. There was no ceiling here, only the open beams of the roof overhead. Charles would be there but in his chair and not allowed to move unless called for a challenge.

Two of the men seemed to be wearing jackets that were a little on the full side. There could be holdouts up the sleeves. He would be especially watchful of any such men.

More players came up the stairs. When all but one were there the man who came up last was the owner of the casino himself, Francis X. Delany.

Charles followed him up the steps and checked his watch.

"Gentlemen, it is five minutes until the appointed hour. Please find chairs at the five tables. Each table will have five players. You all know the rules, no leaving the room or you forfeit the game.

"At each position there is a stack of $15,000 in chips. They are in twenty, fifty, one-hundred and five-hundred dollar amounts. When the final game is down to one table the chip value will be increased to one-thousand, five-thousand and ten-thousand dollars.

"I will be passing along the tables, breaking seals on decks of cards and placing them on the table. Please observe me when I'm at your table so there will be no question.

"Calls for a new deck or a card count are welcomed at any time. Please have one man shuffle the cards as soon as they come to your table and be ready to cut for deal at the stroke of eight o'clock."

Johnny Joe thought of the stacks of money in the safe that could be his, $375,000, and he felt a quiver run through his back. He shook it off, watched one of the men at his table pick up the deck and shuffle it. He would evaluate the men as soon as they began to play.

"Cut the cards for deal, and begin play," Charles said sternly. The games began.

The room was so quiet, Johnny Joe couldn't believe it. He was not at the table with Delany or with the silver king. The ante was established at $50 by a card on each table. All other rules were the same as before.

Johnny Joe didn't think he was nervous, but he failed to raise on a bid when he should have, folded, and the next man raised and won the first pot.

An hour later, Johnny Joe had seen two of the men drop out from the table. They were not poker players, they had come to play only to brag that they had been "in the big game." They splurged their chips and plunged headlong into betting duels between more experienced players with good cards. One of the men wore a cowboy hat, boots and a string tie, but no jacket.

He lost his $15,000 in a little under an hour. The second man was a mouse, did not know when to fold, and bet when it was obvious many times that he could not possibly beat the hand that was on the table. He also probably had all the money he needed and wanted to tell people he had been in on the record game.

And it was a record game! Five more men had tried to get in it, but it had been closed.

At the end of the first hour, Johnny Joe was ahead by about $3,000. It wasn't enough. He had figured out that he couldn't just survive, he had to build up more reserves so when someone bet $20,000 on a hand, he could match it if he had the cards.

Good cards without the depth of finances would cost lots of men their investment tonight.

By the end of the second hour another man dropped out and the third man failed at their table after the third hour.

Charles came and nodded at the two of them left. "If you two gentlemen will come with me, we have another two-man table at the far end."

Johnny Joe surveyed the other tables. Three of them had three players, and two had two. There were thirteen men left out of the 25. He didn't think it would go this fast.

That was just the start. They moved to a table with the silver king and another man who had tiny black eyes, was small and dark, and hardly said a word. The man who came with Johnny Joe was tall and blond, talked too much, but was a master poker player. He seldom made a mistake, and when he did it sometimes worked in his favor.

The next two hours the thirteen men played poker and no one went broke.

"Card count by god!" a man thundered at a table. Charles went to the table, counted the cards, found 55 instead of 52, and asked if any of the three men would prefer to retire from the game. No one moved.

Charles drew his derringer and made a cursory body search. He found no elaborate hold out devices with ropes and steel bars and pulleys.

"If each of you gentlemen would be so kind as to take off your jackets, I will proceed to the next phase of my search," Charles said sternly.

It was as simple as an inside vest pocket.

One of the men swore that he had not added cards to the game. By that time he was the victim whether guilty or not. He was ejected from the game, his chips, some $20,000 worth, would be added 10 percent at a time to the next ten pots. Two armed guards appeared at the top of the stairs from Charles' summons and escorted the still complaining gambler down the steps.

Play continued.

Shortly two more men made their last bets and wandered over to the stairs, took one last look at the remaining players and went down the stairs.

Now there were ten.

Two more tables combined.

Johnny Joe drew a pat hand, a flush of hearts in a game of draw. He held it, raised the bet twice, the last time for $5,000, and only one man stayed.

The pot was worth over $20,000 and Johnny Joe scraped it to his side of the table.

Johnny Joe won the next two hands and estimated that he had about $50,000 on the table in front of him.

"Card count," the silver king said quietly. He had to repeat it so Charles could hear.

"Before the cards are counted," Johnny Joe said, "I propose that the four of us take off our jackets and roll up our sleeves. It's a bit warm in here for me."

Three of the men did so at once, but the fourth man, the small dark one with black eyes, refused.

Charles counted the cards and found 56 pasteboards. The man who had refused to take off his jacket, stood slowly. "I have not cheated," he said clearly.

"Then take off your jacket," Charles said.

"No. It is an affront to my dignity and my honor."

Charles drew the .45 derringer and waved the man aside. "My dignity is backed up with two shots, would you care to challenge them in the next three seconds?"

The man shook his head, turned, and marched out of the room.

Nine players left.

The cheater's stack of chips, about $12,000, was split into ten even stacks and one would be added to each pot.

One table of two had moved to Johnny Joe's which now had a total of five. The only other table had four players.

Francis X. Delany now sat directly across from Johnny Joe. He looked at the men with their jackets off.

"Would you two gentlemen care to join

our informal group with our jackets off?" Johnny Joe asked.

Delany looked up quickly, then nodded. "An excellent idea, then we won't have any more of this card counting nonsense." The two new men removed their jackets and rolled up fancy white shirt sleeves.

The silver king was the next to fall. He tried to bluff Delany when the odds on the cards showing in a seven card stud game were plainly against him. Delany kept raising to the bluff and won the last $5,000 the silver king had. He bet his last $20 chip and called. Delany had his full house and the silver king did not have his straight flush.

Two more men went broke at the table of four, said goodbye, and walked down the stairs. The two remaining men were brought to Johnny Joe's table where they joined the four for a table of six.

The game was down to the last six, the last table.

Johnny Joe checked his watch as the two new men settled in. It was shortly after 3 A.M. Could it be that late? This seemed to be going much faster than he thought it might. He estimated his chips. About $60,000, maybe $65,000. Adequate, but good for only one big loss.

One of the players called for larger chips. Each man bought as many $5,000 chips as he wanted.

The game continued. Johnny Joe checked the players. Delany was a sharp poker player, dedicated to the odds, and a master bluffer. The question was, was he cheating, and if so, how?

The big blond man who had been at Johnny Joe's table from the start, was also an expert player. He tended to over-bet his hand, but that was a common blunder for most players. He was still tough.

The third man around the table was a miner. He wore a plaid shirt, no tie, and had a low crowned slouch hat dropped down his back on a leather thong around his neck. His hands were rough and callous and blistered. He might be a silver millionaire but he still used a pick and shovel.

Delany was across from Johnny Joe and next to him sat a small Chinese man in western clothes. He did a lot of bowing but he knew poker. The last man was so fat he could hardly fit into the chair. His face was heavy with flesh, some crowding his eyes half shut. But his hands were slender and quick. He lounged partly on the table and at one point the far side lifted slightly. He apologized and slid back farther in his chair.

Johnny Joe held the cards when the new men came to the table. He dealt.

It was a game of five card draw and Johnny watched the men closely as they played. So did Delany. He was interested mostly in the two new men, the Chinese and the fat one.

The ante remained at $50 and after looking at his cards, the blond man threw them in without seeing if anyone could open at jacks or better. The miner opened for $1,000, Delany put in his $1,000 and threw away two cards. The Chinese man stayed in, kept two, as did the fat man. Johnny Joe stayed in and retained two cards hoping to strike it lucky and pick up another queen to go with his pair. The miner who opened saved three cards. He was bluffing already.

The miner looked around the circle, then bet $1,000. Everyone stayed in except the fat man who must have decided the openers beat his hand.

The blond man raised $500 and Delany raised another $500. It was $1,000 more to the Chinese man who dropped out and so did Johnny Joe. He figured he was beaten since he had missed his queen.

It was another $500 to the blond man. He called, and then the miner put in his $500 calling Delany. The owner of the casino had three kings and won the hand.

Johnny Joe settled down with some hint as to how the others would play. Most of the men had about $50,000 to $60,000 in front of them. Delany had the most, probably $75,000.

Now Johnny Joe knew. This was when the real poker game began. From here on out to the final call, it would be poker on the best and grandest scale he had ever experienced. Only one tiny spark of doubt plagued him. How in the world was Francis X. Delany cheating? Marked cards? He could have marked a dozen decks and given them to Charles.

"New cards," Johnny Joe said watching Delany closely. The slightly rounded man of sixty-one with the thinning gray hair and liver spots showing on his thin hands did not even look up. He continued to stack chips in front of his pudgy body.

Charles brought the new deck to the table and started to break the seal.

"If I could check the seal," Johnny Joe said. He knew that the seal would have been already delicately removed, probably by steam and later reaffixed perfectly. Johnny Joe examined the seal, then broke it and took the cards out. There were no jokers in these specially made decks. He took off the wrapper and placed the cards on the table top on the ends. He tried to rock them side to side, but they were even and square.

No one had shaved a card here or there to help identify it. All of the cards were the same height. He rubbed his fingers over the back of the cards searching for pin pricks or small bumps. They were flat and smooth. He found the four aces and laid them side by side, with the backs up, then the four kings directly above them. He scanned the figured backs, but could find no printing variance. He held the cards up to the light but found no thumbnail imprints.

He shuffled the cards and handed them to the blond man.

"Look fine to me. If this isn't an honest game, at least from here on out somebody is going to catch a whole lot of hell at breakfast."

There was a murmur of approval as the blond man shuffled the cards three more times since it was a new deck. Then he dealt. Johnny Joe knew it would be seven card stud. The blond's favorite, and he was good at it.

They played for two more hours before the miner tried to bluff Johnny Joe that he had a flush in seven-card. Johnny had put together an ace high straight with only three of the cards showing. He had a pair of aces on the table and had been high through the betting. There was at least $25,000 in the pot and only Johnny Joe and the miner were still playing. The miner made one more bet of $1,000 and Johnny Joe guessed he had pushed the betting as far as he could. He added two $500 chips to the pot and called him.

The miner had been bluffing. He could show only the four clubs and three sevens.

Johnny Joe turned over his ace high straight and took the pot. The miner was down to $150.

The minor swore. "Show down hand for a hundred and fifty?" he asked. Each of the five men put in $150.

The Chinese man won it and the deal. He went back to a hand of draw for the five remaining men.

Johnny Joe shivered as he thought where he was. Playing with the big boys in a game for $375,000! He trembled slightly. He was one of the five men remaining. All he had to do was keep winning and then figure out how Delany was cheating. He must be cheating, but Johnny Joe couldn't figure out how. He watched the man, then looked at Charles, but the cashier was twenty feet away with his back to the game reading a book.

How in hell?

Chapter SIXTEEN

Deputy Sheriff Seth Andrews sat in the police chief's office again.

"You've heard nothing of six men robbing anyone, terrorizing some small town nearby, or blasting a bank wide open? It's been almost two weeks. They must be in hiding. But from what? They don't even know that I'm here looking for them."

The policeman handed over a Wanted poster. It was the one Seth had printed in Oak Park, Texas.

"Yes! Yes, I'm glad to see that it got here. I hope every one of your officers has seen this Wanted and memorized the men's descriptions."

"I doubt if that has happened, Deputy. You see, we have over a thousand Wanted posters. My men can't begin to remember all of the names on them. We don't even refer to them often."

The chief stood, and Seth knew that his little chat with the top policeman in San

Francisco was over.

"We'll do the best we can for you. You work the gambling halls again. You just might get lucky and find them."

Seth went outside and groaned. There were over 200 fairly good sized gambling houses in this town, not to mention 400 or 500 run by the Chinese. He couldn't even find all of them let alone patrol them all.

He would give them another week. If nothing happened, he'd turn tail, get on the boat back to Sacramento, then on the train to the midwest and home to Texas. He'd have to admit that his trip had been a failure.

Damnit to hell! He hated going home empty-handed. He snorted. So much for his own blood oath that he would kill all six of the bastards.

Slightly after 5:30 A.M., Charles came and trimmed the wicks of the four lamps over the upstairs poker table in the El Dorado. They had been playing poker for over nine hours, but Johnny Joe did not feel sleepy. The hot juices of competition were still charging through his bloodstream. During the break, he watched Delany without being observed. The man did nothing that could arouse suspicion. Slowly a single fact filtered through to Johnny Joe.

Perhaps the thrill of the game was still important to the big casino owner. Perhaps he played fair and square, knowing that he was good enough to beat any of them in the preliminaries. He had to play good poker and be a little lucky to get through to the finals, the one-on-one contest.

Once there, if he couldn't win fairly, then he would do his cheating to save all of that money. Yes, reasonable. Now, all Johnny Joe had to do was concentrate on the game at hand.

He did, and two hands later the Chinese man seriously overbet his hand and lost $30,000. He went broke two hands later as the betting now moved into the $5,000 and $10,000 level. The Chinese had lost too easily.

Johnny Joe nodded. The Chinese was a shill, a patsy, one who would get to the last table and then lose and bow out. He might have been playing with Delany's money all along and was supposed to lose now.

Yes, Delany wasn't cheating with cards, he was cheating with ringers, with players.

The fact made Johnny Joe more intense to assure that he would win. He counted cards. He recited odds to himself on every hand of stud. He watched how many cards each of the remaining three players discarded.

For one terrifying, heart-stopping moment, he felt as if he could read each player's mind. But the instant passed and he was glad to be back on the solid ground of reason and observation.

A half hour later the fat man went to sleep in the middle of a hand. They roused him, but he misplayed a simple hand and lost $20,000. On the next hand he bet twice and had nothing in his hand to support it.

At last he shook his head.

"I'm through. I'm sorry. I've got maybe $30,000 here, use it in the next five pots. My apologies for my lack of staying power, and my pleasure to have had the chance to play with such a talented crew. I'll remember this night for the rest of my life."

He stood, bowed and walked over to Charles, gave him some coins and went down the steps.

"So, we are down to three," Delany said. It was his deal. "If there is no objection, why don't we put the gentleman's stake into the pot as a bonus for the winner of this hand?" Both the other men nodded and swept the $30,000 worth of chips into the center.

For the first time in some hours, Johnny Joe examined the chips in front of him. He was slightly ahead of Delany. The blond man had perhaps $20,000 left. He was showing signs of fatigue.

The game was seven card stud. Of the three single cards showing, Delany was high with a ten of spades. He bet $5,000.

The blond man looked up, nodded and put in the five. "Yes, yes. I would do the same thing in your position," the blond said looking at Delany. "Kill off the weakest quickly with big bets. All I have to do is turn the tables on you and win the hand."

The next card up left Johnny Joe with a pair of sevens. Delany had a ten, jack, and the blond had an ace, five.

Johnny Joe bet $3,000, and the blond man grinned, paid it and looked for his third up card. He caught a five of hearts. Johnny Joe raised his third seven, and Delany got a nine. He had a possible straight.

Johnny knew what he had in the hole, a six and a four. He bet $6,000, leaving the blond with only $6,000 left in his stake.

They took the last card down and dirty, and Johnny Joe shuffled it upside down three times before he looked. He saw the six, then checked the next card, the four. The last card was a five. Four legs of a straight, four to seven, which left him with three of a kind, sevens.

"A thousand," Johnny Joe said shoving in a $1,000 chip.

The blond man pushed in a $1,000 chip and looked at Delany.

The casino owner grinned. "Hell, let's get it over with. You either got them or you ain't. I see your $1,000 and I raise $5,000."

"Call," Johnny Joe said dropping in the $5,000. He looked at the blond.

"Like the man said, it's been a pleasure playing with you. Five ain't gonna do me no good. I'll call."

Delany laughed. "What you see is what I got, a damn nothing. Your pot, young man." He held out his hand to the blond. "Nice spending the evening and night playing poker with you. Come back to the El Dorado anytime and there's a hundred dollar chip waiting for you once a week for the next year. Give your name to Charles." Delany hesitated. "Unless I spoke too quickly and you got two more fives in the hole."

"No such luck. Good night, gentlemen." They all stood, the blond shook Johnny Joe's hand and went down the steps.

Charles came over and nodded. "Gentlemen. There is now an option. If both parties agree, there can be a fifteen minute recess for a call to nature. Coffee and sandwiches will be served, if both agree. Otherwise play will continue until one man wins all."

Johnny Joe had not felt the need to relieve himself. He did remember an uncle who said every older man had weak kidneys and some kind of growth that made them prone to frequent urination. He had discounted it at the time. Now as he looked at Delany, he thought it might be of some value.

"Charles, I am perfectly ready to continue play. Coffee this time of morning would nauseate me, I'm afraid. May we have a fresh deck for a fresh game?" As he said it he eased himself in the chair and pulled the twin shot derringer from his pants pocket. He lay it in his lap out of sight under the table just in case he needed it.

Delany showed a quick stab of irritation at Johnny Joe's willingness to continue, then the expression faded and he reached for the new deck. He broke the seal, shuffled it and handed it to Johnny Joe.

"Your deal, I believe."

So it began.

Johnny Joe figured he had about $200,000 in front of him, a mere $25,000 ahead of Delany. Now he would be watching for the cheating. He didn't see how it would be more possible now.

There could be only one method. Somehow, Delany had to know what cards he was holding. By marking the deck, by the use of mirrors, by an accomplice, or some other device. Johnny Joe rejected each of the methods. He played the first hand with his cards held in front of him, but spread wide. Who could see them? How? He had a good hand for draw, three kings. Delany made the opening bet $1,000, but then folded without calling the $10,000 bet. Did he know?

On the second hand Johnny Joe lay his cards on the table in front of them, rubbing his right hand as if it had cramps. He peeked at the cards only to refresh his memory. That time he had a bad hand and played it straight. Delany won the hand but not by cheating.

The next hand Johnny Joe watched Delany's every move. Twice he looked to the left, then let his glance come back to the right until it was almost behind Johnny Joe. This time Johnny Joe held his hand higher and spread wide. He had two pair in the draw poker game and Delany bet $15,000. Johnny folded. Delany knew! He knew he had Johnny beaten. But how?

They played another half dozen hands. Each time Johnny brought his cards up high, Delany dumped his hand, or he bet big dollars. He knew what cards Johnny Joe had and if he could win or not.

Slowly the realization came. *Behind him.* There was someone behind him. But it was a blank wall. A small peephole and a telescope could do it if the player held his hand up to be seen.

Again he lifted his hand and from the corner of his eye watched Delany. When Delany looked behind Johnny Joe, he snapped his head around. Two red sticks lowered slowly from a small window almost directly behind Johnny Joe.

Johnny Joe had the derringer in his right hand as he whirled. Instantly, he fired one shot at the two-foot-square glass window. The derringer's .45 bite barked loudly in the hall, and brought up Charles in a rush.

The glass shattered and Johnny Joe was on his feet in a second racing around the poker tables to the small window in the side wall. He broke out more of the glass with the butt of the pistol and pushed it through into the false wall of the room.

A small man sat on a chair shaking. Blood seeped from a glass cut on his cheek. He held two red sticks. On a table beside him were six more of different colors. In front of him was a twenty power telescope aimed through a hole in the wall.

"Come out of there or you're a dead man," Johnny Joe snarled.

The man pushed a lever and slipped out of a concealed three foot high door.

Johnny Joe marched the man back to the table where Delany sat with his hands covering his face.

"Charles, I think you have a duty to perform here," Johnny Joe said sharply.

"I beg your pardon, Mr. Williams?"

"We have caught a cheater red handed with an accomplice, a telescope and sticks used to signal what cards I was holding. The cheater, like the others we've had tonight, is in default and must leave the contest."

"But . . . but it's the final match, the final two!"

"Even more reason it must be honest. I've been trying to figure out how you cheated me before in one of the nightly games, Delany. It must have been this way. Now I see. You play good poker, Delany. There was no reason for you to cheat. You haven't until now. Not when someone facing toward that wall could see the window and the sticks. Oh, no, you saved it for the final victim.

"Charles, I'll take the $375,000 in cash, all gold coins. You have it safely in your vault. Call two of your security guards to help me verify the count. I'll also want two San Francisco policemen to be on hand to escort me back to the San Francisco Bank."

"Williams . . ." Delany began.

"Delany, I see no reason to make this cheating episode public. I'll be staying in town, however, and playing in your games from time to time. If I ever hear or find any cheating of any kind in this game, by you, I'll sign a complaint with the chief of police against you."

"No need to get dramatic, young man. You play good poker. You are intelligent and quick. You can realize that I'm a gambler. I gambled on a small cheating device that failed. Most gamblers cheat. I lost. I can accept that. There will be no attempt made to interfere with you collecting your money. After all, only $15,000 of it was mine."

"Not so, Mr. Delany. The Chinese and at least one more man tonight were your shills, playing with your entry money. They lost when you signaled them to lose. You cheated two ways."

"Well, well. You are sharper than I expected. Now, it's late and my bladder is about to explode. The old man's disease. If you will excuse me."

Charles collected the chips and put them away, then led Johnny Joe downstairs. The guards were there. In the vault, Johnny Joe looked at the resources of the El Dorado. He accepted ten pound bars of gold in lieu of coins for part of the payment.

They didn't have it counted out until almost noon. A special armored wagon came from the bank. They loaded on 30 ten-pound bars of gold worth $99,220. Then bags of coins for the $275,780 balance. That was 13,789 twenty dollar double eagles.

The coins alone weighed 862 pounds. Once the money was in the bank, the papers filled out and deposit receipts given, and the bank was astounded and thankful, Johnny Joe took a cab home to his room and fell into his bed.

Only then did he realize that it was Sunday afternoon. The bank had opened especially for him to make his deposit.

What he didn't realize yet was that he was a rich man.

Chapter SEVENTEEN

When Johnny Joe left the bank it was nearly noon and he was so tired he could hardly think straight. He failed to notice the two men getting into a black buggy and following him when he caught a hack outside the bank. At the hotel, one of the men hurried into the lobby just after Johnny Joe did and stepped into the elevator with him and two other people.

When Johnny Joe got off on the sixth floor, so did the man following him. He turned the opposite way down the hall that Johnny Joe did. He watched the young gambler and when he turned into room 610, the follower walked back that way to make sure of the room number. He heard the door close and lock.

A few moments later the follower was downstairs talking to the second man in the buggy. Charles, the steward, banker and referee at the big poker match, frowned for just a moment, then shrugged and dismissed the follower and the buggy and walked into the hotel.

He made his way to the sixth floor up the stairs and paused to catch his breath. He walked down to room 610 and took three skeleton keys from his pocket. Most hotel door locks were stupidly simple to get through. He saw that no one was in the hall and tried two of his keys quietly on room 610. The third one turned the lock and he edged the door in cautiously. Nothing sat in front of it.

Charles stepped into the room silently, took a six-inch stiletto from his boot and advanced on the sleeping figure on the bed.

Johnny Joe had fallen on the bed on his stomach and gone to sleep at once. Later he rolled over to his back. He lay there, still dressed, snoring peacefully. The long stiletto came down viciously as Charles stabbed Johnny Joe in the heart. His body shook, he half rose, his eyes misted and then the blade came down again through his blood pump and ripped out sideways.

The blade tore through three sections of the heart, stopping it immediately. Johnny Joe Williams spasmed once more, one hand lifted then fell and he gave one long last sigh as the air gushed out of his dead lungs.

Charles watched the death throes, then

wiped the blade on Johnny Joe's expensive jacket and pushed the stiletto back in his boot. He went to the door, made certain no one was in the hall, then slipped out and walked quickly to the stairs and went down. He met no one on the steps. He walked out of the hotel by the nearest door.

Two hours later, in a restaurant, Willy Boy heard the news that the big poker game was over. The great Francis X. Delany had been whipped by some kid from New Orleans. The kid's name was Johnny Joe Williams and he won $375,000. Willy Boy almost tipped over his soup. He left the eatery without finishing his dinner and ran the four blocks back to the hotel and hurried up to Johnny Joe's room.

None of them had wanted to see if he was back when they got up that morning. They had been afraid that he had lost and wouldn't want to talk about it.

He had won!

Willy Boy knocked on the door of room 610, but got no response. He turned the door knob and when he found it unlocked he hurried into the room.

The pool of blood on Johnny Joe's shirt told him the story at once. He touched his cooling body, tried for a pulse. None. He leaned against the wall and stared at his dead friend. What now? What should he do next? Get his people away so the police couldn't question them? Yes. What else? The poke. The twelve thousand in gold and greenbacks they had taken in the mine holdup.

Johnny Joe said win or lose it should be divided up among the men. He hadn't needed it. It was rightfully theirs. Willy Boy nodded, pulled out Johnny Joe's carpetbag and hefted it. The gold must be inside. He checked, found it and the paper money. It would all be there. He took the carpetbag and stepped outside after one final look at his dead friend.

The rest of the gang had to get out of the hotel. There was a chance that the police might know their names. He found Gunner and Juan in their rooms and told them to pack and leave the hotel at once and meet in front of the El Dorado gambling hall. The police could be coming any minute.

"The El Dorado is closed today," Juan said.

"That's fine, get out of here as soon as you can, five minutes. Move, now!"

Willy Boy went back to his room and packed. He took the gold and paper money from Johnny Joe's carpetbag and put it in his own. They could divide it later. Then he wondered where Eagle and the Professor were. He finished packing his own gear and left it ready to move.

Then he searched every eating place within two blocks. He couldn't find Eagle and the Professor.

As he searched he knew who had killed Johnny Joe, or had him killed. The cheating gambler who couldn't stand to be whipped at his own table, Francis X. Delany was the killer. The gambler would die. There was no room for discussion or argument. First he had to get his people safely away from that hotel.

He sat in the lobby waiting for them. The late editions of the Sunday paper had a story on the biggest poker game of the century. And it said that Johnny Joe Williams of New Orleans was the winner. If Deputy Seth Andrews was in town he would begin canvassing the hotels to find Johnny Joe.

Willy Boy paced the lobby waiting. He was there for an hour before the two men strolled in. He grabbed them, hustled them into the elevator and explained to them why they had to move.

"Dead? Johnny Joe got killed?" Eagle asked, pain and disbelief on his face.

"A knife, possibly while he was sleeping.

No struggle, he was still fully dressed like he just came back from the game."

"He took the gold to the bank first," the Professor said. "They opened the bank special on Sunday for him to deposit all that gold."

The two men packed, took their carpetbags and went down the stairs and out the side entrance. They had paid for a week in advance when they arrived.

At the El Dorado, the three picked up Juan and Gunner and told them that Johnny Joe was dead. They couldn't believe it.

"He wins a fortune and then somebody kills him?" Gunner asked. "That's not fair."

Willy Boy paced the sidewalk as they moved down the street.

"Where does this Francis Delany live? That we need to know first. Where is he right now? Is there a back door to the casino?"

The Professor nodded grimly. "We forget about robbing one of the casinos, right? Instead we settle up with Delany."

"Absolutely," Willy Boy said. He looked around. "I didn't think I even had to ask. He hurt our team, now we pay him back. Has to be done." The other four men nodded.

"The faster we can work, before they find Johnny Joe, the better for us. Juan, you and Gunner go back to your hotel room and box up as much of that trail food and gear as you can. Then get a hack and drive it out to the livery stable where Eagle rented those horses. He can tell you where it is.

"The Professor and Eagle and I will find out all we can about Delany, as fast as we can."

They all left on their missions. They would all meet at a fountain two blocks down from the El Dorado as soon as they had done their job or had enough information about Delany.

Willy Boy started in a cafe down from the El Dorado. He asked questions about the gambler. Soon he found where the man lived. A big house on Nob Hill.

He asked other places but no one knew the address. Willy Boy went back to the fountain and waited. He had a way they could learn the man's address once they got in the area.

An hour later, the Professor came back, and then Eagle. It was nearly four in the afternoon.

"He lives on Nob Hill, and went to church today," the Professor reported. "But someone heard him say he was feeling ill and would be home most of the day."

"He's going to feel worse than he thinks he does."

Eagle came back with the man's address. They decided that just after dark would be best.

"I hear he lives alone in a big house and has servants in during the day," Eagle said.

"Let's use the horses," the Professor advised. "Make an easier, quicker getaway."

They hired a cab and rode out to the livery barn and found Gunner and Juan sorting, packing and loading the camping gear and food into saddlebags and gunny sacks.

They finished the job quickly, reluctantly bought two more horses from the same livery and saddled up and rode out just before dark. People turned to stare at them as they rode into the better part of town. They were the real Wild West, with rifles in boots, bedrolls and carpetbags on the back of the saddles.

Eagle had directions to the Nob Hill section and the house number. Well before they got there, Willy Boy held up his hand and they rode into a vacant lot and gathered around him.

"Five of us is too many. We'll take only three. Gunner, Eagle and me. You other two will watch the horses and keep us ready to leave in a hurry. Let's move up closer, then the three of us will do the last block on foot."

They left the horses with Juan and the Professor a block and a half away on a vacant lot that had three trees growing on it.

Willy Boy and Gunner both had sawed off shotguns they carried against their chests. Eagle had his six-gun. They checked the front of the house, went between lots to the alley and up to the same house's back door. It was unlocked.

The three cocked hammers on shotguns and pistols and slipped into the back door to a small entryway. Beyond that was a kitchen. Voices came from a room down a thirty foot hall. They slid along the hall, watching both ways. Willy Boy led them, Eagle had the rear.

Willy Boy looked into a lighted room and nodded. Two men sat in chairs before a blaze in a beautiful fireplace. Johnny Joe had told them that Delany was over 60. Willy Boy figured he was the one on the left. The other one was not over 30.

Willy Boy stepped into the room and lifted the sawed off double barreled scatter gun.

"Gentlemen!" he barked.

Both men jumped and turned toward him.

"Keep your hands in sight and don't say a word. Let me introduce myself. I'm Willy

Boy, and Johnny Joe Williams was the best friend I ever had. You two killed him."

The other two Outlaws came out, circled around and made sure neither man had a weapon.

"Stand up!" Willy Boy barked.

Both men stood, the younger one looking at the older man. Eagle and Gunner had closed the doors leading into the room so that no one could shoot them from behind.

"Why did you kill him, Delany?" Willy Boy growled.

"I didn't touch him. I didn't kill anyone." Delany's chin began to quiver.

"You didn't have to, you told one of your people to kill him, probably this one here. I'm going to start whittling on your fingers until you remember who you ordered to do your murdering for you."

Willy Boy let the shotgun down and Gunner lifted his. Willy Boy took out his knife and touched the blade, then pushed the older man back into his chair and put his hand palm down on the heavy wooden arm of the chair. Before the man could react, Willy Boy drove the half-inch wide blade through the back of Delany's hand and into the wood.

Delany bellowed in rage. The younger man fainted to the floor. Gunner kicked him in the side until he came back to consciousness.

"Stand him up," Willy Boy said. Gunner lifted him to his feet where he swayed from side to side but didn't fall.

"Now, Delany. Who did you order to kill my best friend?"

The old man's face had gone white. Blood seeped from his hand onto the chair's arm and ran down the side dripping onto the expensive upholstery.

He looked at the blood, then up at Willy Boy.

"I told this man here, Charlie, my head cashier. I told him to kill the man who beat me at my own game of winner take all."

Willy Boy caught Gunner's knife by the handle when the big man tossed it. This was a fighting knife, ten inches of blade two inches wide with a good groove and a three inch point sharpened on both sides.

Willy Boy put the point against Charlie's throat.

"Tell me, Charlie. Did you kill my best friend with your knife?"

The man swallowed, bringing a gasp of pain as the blade drew a drop of blood. He tried to look down at the knife. Then he looked at Willy Boy.

"Yes. Delany said he would fire me if I didn't. He's been my boss for ten years."

Willy Boy stepped back. "This court finds both of you guilty of the murder of Johnny Joe Williams of New Orleans. You both are sentenced to death. The sentence is to be carried out at once."

Willy Boy stepped back, drew the blade from the old man's hand, carefully wiped the blood off on Delany's white shirt and returned the knife to his boot.

"Stand up, Delany. You've lived like a bastard, at least you can die like a man."

Delany stood. "Don't do this. I'm a rich man. I can give you each $100,000. You'll never have to work another day in your life."

Willy Boy hit him in the mouth with the barrel of his shotgun. Blood splattered and broken teeth flew. Delany slumped against Charlie.

"Never try to bribe an honest man, Delany." Willy Boy drew his pistol and without a pause shot Delany in the right knee. Gunner shot Charlie in his left knee. Both men crashed to the floor. Blood poured from the wounds. The men screamed in pain and torment.

"You'll never kill another innocent man, Delany. You got too greedy, too self important. You were a big man, but now you're just another hunk of meat bleeding into your expensive rug."

Willy Boy shot him in the other knee. Eagle shot Charlie in the shoulder.

The sound of the six-guns going off filled the room with a roaring that was followed by billows of blue smoke from the black powder. When it rose a little toward the ceiling, Willy Boy stared at the fire and he nodded.

He lifted the shotgun and pointed it at Delany who lay sprawled on the floor not trying to stop the blood from either wound.

"Say your last prayers, Delany," Willy Boy said. Then he fired the charge of buckshot from four feet into the gambler's chest. Gunner executed Charlie the same way, then all three men emptied their six-guns into the men's chests.

Willy Boy wiped sweat from his forehead, then grabbed a burning stick from the fireplace and lit the fancy curtains. Eagle did the same in the other rooms.

By the time the three men left by the back door, the whole house was blazing with fire.

They heard pounding on the front door and voices calling, but by then they were walking down the alley away from the structure.

The five remaining members of the Willy Boy Gang hit leather and rode calmly out of San Francisco south along the big bay.

★ ★ ★

The next day at the San Francisco police station, Deputy Seth Andrews showed the flyer to every policeman he could talk to. Yes, Johnny Joe Williams was one of the men he sought, but now he wanted the other five. At last he got in to see the chief.

"Isn't it plain? They found their friend dead and went after the only man who could have killed him, Francis Delany. The other five members of the Willy Boy Gang are the ones who slaughtered those two men on Nob Hill."

The police chief nodded. "Probably, but we have no evidence, not one witness, not one bit of proof."

"You don't need any. You have my warrant for all five of them. Release to the newspapers the story about the papers you found on Johnny Joe. Just a straight story that this Johnny Joe had papers naming Willy Boy Lambier and the Professor as cosigners of Johnny Joe's account at the bank. All they have to do is go to the bank, write their names on a signature card and they can withdraw all $375,000."

"Yes, I see, that kind of story might get them back there in a rush, or get them out of hiding. I'll think about it." The chief preened his moustache. "You'd have to make your own arrangements with the bank to notify you in case they come back."

"Easy enough to do. In fact, I'll do it the moment you release the story to the newspapers."

"Yes, I'll think about it," the chief said.

Willy Boy and his four men rode south around the long arm of San Francisco Bay and then worked east. When they were clear of the mud flats, they turned north again and headed for Sacramento. They were in no hurry. They had enough money to last a year if they wanted to lay low.

But they wouldn't.

On the fourth day they passed a small town, and the Professor made a quick stop to get a San Francisco newspaper so he could keep up with the national and world news.

Willy Boy laughed. "What difference does it make? How are you going to change the world? Better we don't let anybody see any of us. That damn Deputy Seth Andrews could be out here checking on us."

That night around the campfire, Willy Boy told them what he had decided. "We'll get up to Sacramento and test the waters and see if there are ten or fifteen posse members looking for us. If not, we'll get on the train and head for Denver.

"Our good friend the Professor says he knows of a bank there that is just begging to be taught a lesson. This time I hope he doesn't get shot up the way he did the first time."

The Professor grinned. "Damn well will be a different tune this time around. We do it right, we blow hell out of their guards and we take off with all the loot we can carry. Damn, I been waiting for this chance to get back at those bastards for almost two years!"

Gunner looked at the fire and wiped a tear from his cheek. "Sure miss Johnny Joe. Wish he was with us."

"We all miss Johnny Joe," the Professor said. "But he died about as happy as a man can, I'd say. He reached the pinnacle of his life. He beat that bastard Delany fair and square. He went out on top of the heap."

Willy Boy nodded and leaned back. Speaking about being on top of the heap, he wouldn't be until he killed the man who had murdered his father. He was probably still in Kansas. One of these days he'd find that bastard. One of these days.

Juan missed Johnny Joe as well, but they all knew the chances they took. Now he was looking forward to getting closer to Mexico. Soon he would be there with his wife Juanita and little Ernesto.

Eagle threw a piece of wood in the fire. He was playing out the string. The others had helped him achieve the big dream of his life, now it was his turn to see that they had a chance for their moments of glory.

The Professor started to relax by reading a copy of the San Francisco *Statesman*. He had found the paper along the roadway. Someone had torn off the front page. Soon he tired of reading and threw it aside. The paper flipped open to a headline on top of page six:

"Friends of Slain big Winner
Can Claim his $375,000 Jackpot"

None of the Willy Boy Gang saw the story. The next morning they broke camp and rode north for Sacramento, and then Denver.

The next day the murder and the free $375,000 was old news, even for the Sacramento newspaper that the Professor digested. The Professor threw down the newspaper and thought about Denver. He knew he was going to be smiling every mile of the way!

The employees of Thorndike Press hope you have enjoyed this Large Print book. All our Thorndike and Wheeler Large Print titles are designed for easy reading, and all our books are made to last. Other Thorndike Press Large Print books are available at your library, through selected bookstores, or directly from us.

For information about titles, please call:

(800) 223-1244

or visit our Web site at:

www.gale.com/thorndike
www.gale.com/wheeler

To share your comments, please write:

Publisher
Thorndike Press
295 Kennedy Memorial Drive
Waterville, ME 04901